DEATH IS A GRIZZLY

By J.C. Graves

Summit Bay Press, Olympia WA

i

To my brother, Peter Graves,
who introduced me to westerns by
giving me the book *Flint* by Louis L'Amour.

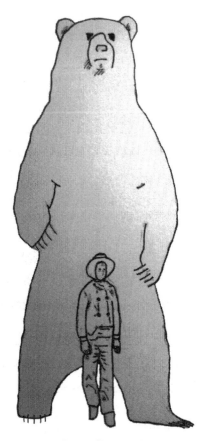

Great Bear is 16 feet tall, the man 6.
Kodiak grizzlies and polar bears have
reached 10 feet tall.

CHAPTER ONE

Large snowflakes drifted down, forming a thick white blanket over the valley. The first big snow of the season cast the mountains in wintery beauty. As the sun set behind the tall pines, the elk herd entered the familiar meadow to bed down for the night. The large bull lifted his nose, swinging his head left and right. He caught the faint whiff of something undefined. He snorted and scanned the forest carefully, but nothing moved. He huffed again to show his agitation. He needed more information. What was it? Most of the herd seemed unconcerned, although some of the cows watched him with mild interest. They sensed nothing. He trumpeted loudly—a challenge. If wolves were near, he would lower his great rack and charge into them. He stomped the ground irritably.

Great Bear watched all of this with practiced patience, downwind of the herd. He had been on the edge of the meadow, behind thick brush, since before the latest snow began to fall. Now he was completely covered and invisible to the herd, except his dark, deep-set, brooding eyes. An old cow wandered over to the south side of the meadow. She watched the bull elk bugle and stomp but did not sense or smell immediate danger. She was old and tired and lay down heavily.

Great Bear exploded from the wood line like an avalanche of powdered snow. In two bounds he was on the frightened cow before she had a chance to stand. He rolled her over onto her back and tore out the throat in one vicious bite. The herd scattered. Over the next two hours, Great Bear gorged himself on the lean flesh, leaving little more than bones and hide. The local wolf clan howled off to the east and would arrive soon to clean up the remains, not that he would leave them much.

When he finished, he stood on hind legs, sniffing the air. Two ravens landed in the cedar tree and squawked. They wanted to get as much elk scraps as possible before the wolves arrived. He glanced at them briefly through the thickening snow flurries. Winter had arrived in force and his ancient cave was not far off. The idea of a nice long sleep was all he cared about now.

Little Turtle was a mighty warrior, at least in his own eyes. At twelve, he could ride well and had helped defend the village from the Pawnee raid last autumn. He had fired his arrow at a Pawnee warrior, striking him in the chest, but not a mortal wound. When the angry man ran at him with his knife, his uncle pushed him out of the way and killed the attacker. He would ride better, he thought, if only he had his own horse. He had helped in the last buffalo hunt. Everyone participated. It was a tribal event—if you wanted to eat, you worked. The warriors rode into the herd, firing arrows and rifles at point blank range, while the boys followed and speared the wounded buffalo. He had been covered in blood just like Black Spotted Horse—the chief's only son—a year older but with his own horse. They ate the liver and felt like mighty warriors, boasting of their many accomplishments and hunting prowess.

But he did not care for his name, mainly because of the teasing he had to endure from some of the older boys. "What did he need to do to have a man's name?" he asked.

His uncle, White Crow, replied, "Turtle does not worry if it is turtle; eagle does not worry if it is eagle. Worry not about such things. You will discover your name like we all do."

"I will *discover* my name? What does that even mean?" In a way, he knew exactly what it meant, but he was impatient, as usual. He did not want to wait for the testing or something accidental to happen. He thought of Thunder Cloud, one of the chiefs. How did he get that name? Was he on the prairie when the storm swept by? Did someone hear him bellow loudly like the tall summer clouds?

White Crow noticed the doubtful look. "We earn our names by our actions, or our new names are given to us after the testing, or it just comes as you meditate on the Great Spirit."

The boy's shoulders slumped.

White Crow studied the boy's downcast features. He huffed lightly. To be a boy again, he thought wistfully. As a boy he had not worried about anything, but Little Turtle seemed to worry about everything. Maybe that was just his nature. Every tribe needed at least one person who worried, to keep everyone a little more alert and conscious of possible dangers. Most of the time the worries did not materialize, but when that one time finally happened, the constant worrying was justified — at least for the moment. "What name would you choose for yourself?"

Little Turtle looked up in surprise. He had not thought of it. Big Wolf came to mind first, but it didn't *feel* right. He shrugged and walked away. What name did he want?

Around the fire each evening, the People ate and talked and told stories. The warriors planned their next hunt. Until the buffalo arrived, they would move up into the hills to bring back elk and moose.

"But not the hills to the south," Chief Eagle Soars said firmly.

"No," White Crow agreed. "Not those hills."

As they walked back to their lodge, Little Turtle asked, "Why do we not hunt those hills?"

"Great Bear makes his home there," his uncle replied, waving his hand toward the southwest.

Great Bear, Little Turtle thought. His mind raced ahead with possible ideas. That would make an excellent name. He wanted that name. He didn't tell anyone his plan.

He began practicing with his bow every day until he grew strong enough to use a man's bow and hit small targets with every shot. He made a new bow that was even stronger. He would kill Great Bear with one shot to the heart or head and make a necklace of the long, black claws.

The People watched his daily practice and how he improved, and said he would become a great warrior and hunter. From short distances he was more accurate than the warriors using rifles.

"Can I try your new bow," Black Spotted Horse asked.

Part of Little Turtle was annoyed at the question, but another part felt proud at the show of interest. Without a word, he handed it to his friend.

Black Spotted Horse pulled back the string, but his right arm shook a little. "Why did you make it so hard to pull back?"

"Here, let me show you." Little Turtle took the bow. "See that box the army rifles came in?" Black Spotted Horse nodded. The box was standing on end. "Well, it is far and the wood is thick." He nocked an arrow, pulled the string back to his right ear, and let the arrow fly. "Come on." They jogged the eighty feet to the box.

Little Turtle pointed to the back. "Look here."

"Oh," Black Spotted Horse said, surprised. "Your arrow went through the lid *and* the back of the box."

"The bows everyone use can hit the box, but none can go through *both* pieces of wood. My arrow goes through both. And look from how far away."

Black Spotted Horse was impressed. "Why didn't the arrow head break on the hard wood?"

"My arrow heads are a little thicker and longer." He knew he would never get the arrow shaft out of the box, where two others were lodged. So he broke off the tip and gave it to Black Spotted Horse for closer inspection.

Without looking up from the arrowhead, Black Spotted Horse said, "My sister thinks you will be a chief someday."

Little Turtle's ears turned red. He had been secretly watching Shouts At The Wind. They had played together as children, but now she was turning into a young woman and did the chores of a young woman of the village. He thought she was the most beautiful of them all, although she had a well-known temper. He didn't care about things like that; he just wanted her. If he killed Great Bear, she would surely want him too.

In the afternoon he watched her walk out of the village to the spring. Without seeming too obvious, he followed. When out of sight of the village, he broke into a light jog. He arrived at the spring as she finished chopping a hole in the ice and pushed the basket under the water. The village women wove baskets of prairie sweetgrass so tight, they could carry water. He watched her fill it, loving the form of her kneeling on the rocks. When she stood, he stepped out of the reeds.

"Oh!" she said, surprised. But she really wasn't. When she left the village, she had watched Little Turtle from the corner of her eye. When she knelt to pluck a dry white flower, she noticed him watching her and turned toward the spring. But this was the game the young people played, since the beginning of time.

He didn't offer to carry the heavy basket; that was women's work. But he walked beside her, his face grim and serious. She glanced at him and smiled. He noticed her head turn toward him and looked at her. He had to smile too. Then they laughed together.

He loved the sound of her laugh: light and tinkling. "Do you want to come watch me shoot rabbits with my bow? I kill more rabbits than anyone, because I can shoot them from farther away."

She loved the sound of his laugh; the way his voice broke when he tried to speak. His voice was changing from the high boy voice to the deep man voice. "After I gather wood," she replied softly.

He felt giddy. He wanted to help her gather wood so they could leave quickly, but that was also woman's work. He would make more arrowheads while he waited.

They crept through the sage, soundless on moccasin feet, peering over and around the brush and boulders.

He killed two rabbits. "These are for you," he said proudly, trying to sound like an adult. She squealed with delight each time and carried them by the ears

A loud thrashing from behind the thicket made them turn around. Across the small meadow, an old bull buffalo grunted and broke from the brush, charging with head down.

The bull was coming too fast and they were still in the open. "Run away from the bull!" he shouted.

Without a word, she turned and sprinted away, dropping the rabbits on the ground. Little Turtle ran sideways from the bull's path, hoping to draw it away from her. He thought he could probably outrun the bull by zigzagging, when he got into the trees. As the bull veered toward him, he automatically pulled an arrow out of the quiver in case he needed it.

Shouts At The Wind tripped and fell, sliding on the wet grass. "Oh!" she called. Without slowing, the bull turned back to her.

Little Turtle fit the arrow and pulled the gut string back to his right ear. He hesitated half a second to steady his aim and let loose. The arrow slammed into the bull's chest just behind the right elbow, buried to the nock. The front legs collapsed and folded under. The great shaggy chin plowed into the prairie as the beast slid to a stop and toppled over onto its left side, tongue hanging out. The old bull thrashed its legs a few times, then let out a final steamy breath and became quiet.

Shouts At The Wind stood, shakily, hands clenching and unclenching nervously. The bull's head was only four feet from her, eyes glazing over. She looked wildly at the bull then Little Turtle and back again. She ran to him, wrapping her arms around his neck, and sobbed. She clung to him tightly until the tension slowly released. Finally, they just enjoyed holding each other, foreheads and noses touching.

Shouts At The Wind stepped back, grinning shyly. She took out her knife and deftly removed the bull's big tongue, waving the prize in the air and laughing. "I cook for you!" she said fiercely, her eyes wild with delight. She jumped up and ran to the village, shouting that Little Turtle killed a buffalo with one arrow and saved her life.

The village descended on the kill. The warriors wanted to see what had actually happened, but the women came prepared to butcher the prize of fresh meat.

Red Wolf knelt by the bull, fingering the nock of the arrow, sticking out of the hide only one inch. He was impressed: it was a killing blow and had penetrated into the heart and beyond. He had been alive forty-one winters and had been on many hunts. He had never heard of anyone killing a full-grown bull with one arrow—maybe a rifle, but not an arrow. To kill a big bull usually took many arrows, or spears, or rifles. He had seen rifles kill a bull with one shot to the head. He stood back admiring the kill. His wife, Jumping Antelope, knelt in front of him and cut downward past the ribs to free the arrow. She tugged but it remained fast. She looked up at him. He stepped forward, reaching into the meat, and yanked three times before the arrow came out.

Now he was impressed again. The arrow shaft was longer than others by at least six inches, the arrow head fatter and longer by almost two inches, and the feathers were longer but trimmed closer to the perfectly straight shaft. He looked around. Little Turtle stood behind everyone, watching Red Wolf closely. Red Wolf waved him over.

"Very good," he said simply, handing the bloody arrow to Little Turtle.

Little Turtle just nodded. Red Wolf was the greatest hunter in the tribe. Any praise from him was like a warm blanket on a cold night. Refreshing. Exhilarating.

"Your bow?" He held his hand out.

Little Turtle handed it to him, his brow wrinkled in concentration, worried about the inspection. Except for

Black Spotted Horse, no one else had showed any interest in what he had been doing, or what he had created through much trial and error.

Red Wolf easily pulled the string back to his right cheek and held it there for a count of three, then slowly released it, nodding satisfactorily. Little Turtle handed him the bloody arrow. Forty yards away the grove of cottonwoods stood like sentinels behind the meadow. He found a dark mark on the mostly white tree, aimed and fired. The arrow flew true, striking just above a small dark patch on the bark, six feet off the ground.

He handed the bow to Little Turtle, nodding his head toward the tree. "You."

Little Turtle suppressed a smile, with effort. He fit an arrow, aimed and fired, all in one fluid movement, barely pausing to aim. His arrow hit the dark part of the bark in the center. Now he did smile, looking at Red Wolf.

Red Wolf smiled also. "Good." He meant excellent. He meant exceptional. But he was a man of few words.

They walked together to the tree to retrieve the arrows. Red Wolf pulled out his arrow, examining the arrow head closely. He grunted with satisfaction. The arrowhead was still perfect. He handed it to Little Turtle.

"You hunt with men now," Red Wolf said. Before Little Turtle could respond, he turned and walked toward the village.

Little Turtle's head swam. Red Wolf was treating him like a man, inviting him to do a man's job.

After the elk hunt, the warriors did not go back out, so Little Turtle did not have the opportunity to hunt with the men. Occasionally, someone would bring in an antelope, but mostly they were living off dried meat, dried berries, and acorn bread, waiting for the buffalo to return in the spring.

CHAPTER TWO

Months later, as winter began to fade and the days grew longer and warmer, Little Turtle sat by the little fire with Shouts At The Wind. She knew it would not help, but she had to try one more time. "But I don't want you to go," she pleaded.

He stared into the fire, his mind made up. He held his hands to the fire until they started to hurt, then quickly grabbed her hands. She flinched at the sudden movement and sudden heat.

"Inside, I am hot, like this." He shook their hands together. "Burning up. I want to prove myself a warrior, not just a bull killer. I want to walk proud. With a name like no other. We are not old enough to marry, but in a few years we will be together. And you will be proud of me."

"But you are already a great warrior," she declared with conviction. "You saved me, and I am proud of you now."

He frowned. If only that was enough. He could not get Great Bear out of his mind. They had this argument before. She knew he planned to leave but not when. It would be easier if he left without telling her. If she clung to him, he might lose his resolve. Most of the older women watched their husbands leave without making a fuss. It was the younger ones who often wept, even if they tried to hide it. Fighting was a man's work, and he would not shy away from the task he had assigned to himself.

In early spring before first light, Little Turtle quietly departed the village, easily avoiding the two night guards. He carried his bow, a quiver of ten arrows he had made, a knife, a blanket, and a bag of dried buffalo and antelope meat, and dried berries. He did not know exactly where he was going—somewhere in the Great Bear mountains—but he knew where to start.

On the second day of his journey, a late season storm blanketed the prairie with a quarter-inch of snow. He sat on the rocky knoll and watched the small herd of twenty-six buffalo down in the river valley. The sky was clear and the sun felt good on his back. The snow would be gone by afternoon, he thought. He did not notice the wolf pack slowly working its way along the east side of the herd, toward him.

The prairie was quiet and peaceful. The green grass was already an inch tall, and the first yellow and white wildflowers were opening. The sounds of the herd traveled up the hill with the usual snorts and gruntings. Two of the young bulls pushed each other around. A meadow lark called and flitted from one bush to another. Another meadow lark in the distance answered. A covey of quail hunted seeds in the streambed down on the right, calling in their unique language: a sound that warmed his heart. Quail and blackbirds with red wings, he thought, make the best sounds. Off to his left rear, a ground squirrel chirped a warning. At the squirrel's alert signal, he turned his head slowly, expecting to see a hawk drifting into the area. The big wolf surprised him.

The pack of gray wolves had been stalking the buffalo herd for several weeks. They were patient, knowing that the spring calves and the old bulls and cows would make themselves readily available. Such had been the life and death struggle they had participated in for centuries. A shortage of food had not been a problem. The pack usually chose calves or cows, because even an old bull could be dangerou. But they had not eaten in six days. With empty stomachs, they were maneuvering into position to make a fresh kill.

The big gray wolf did not expect to see a lone human, sitting out on the prairie. Normally he avoided humans. They had weapons that could kill from a distance. Still, a lone human tempted him: they were soft and slow. Out of curiosity, he turned toward the figure. Maybe it was wounded, or old and dying.

Little Turtle stood slowly, letting the blanket fall from his wide shoulders. He carefully, but not in a rush, strung his bow and fitted an arrow. He could see the whole pack now—eight other wolves, working their way down the valley, behind but parallel to the small herd. This lone wolf must have been scouting the far flank and discovered him by accident. If he killed this wolf, would the pack come to investigate? Probably, because the wolf would howl in pain before he died. He glanced from the wolf back toward the pack. It didn't matter. Now that he had stood, they also spotted him and were turning in his direction. Running was out of the question. He sighed in resignation, a cloud of vapor breath filling the cold, dry air in front of him. He shrugged lightly; he had enough arrows, if it came to that. And he felt no fear.

When the wolf was well within his range, he raised the bow, aimed the arrow and shouted, "Stop!"

The wolf stopped, as if trained. After a few seconds, it lowered its head, and with a low, rumbling growl began cautiously walking toward him.

He did not want to kill the wolf, but he would, if forced to. He also knew he could kill the whole pack with his powerful bow and perfect arrows, if he had to. While still aiming, he stepped purposefully toward the wolf and it stopped again.

This was different, the wolf thought. This human was prepared to fight and had even stepped toward him. He glanced back toward the pack, down the sloping prairie to his left. They were coming at a trot.

When the wolf glanced back at the pack, Little Turtle did too. The pack had started to lope toward them. If he did not act soon, he would be surrounded—an easy meal. If anyone found his bones, they would assume he had been foolish and deserved this terrible death.

He made a quick decision. He ran at the wolf, bow at the ready. The wolf stopped abruptly then retreated a few steps in confusion. Little Turtle kept chasing the wolf, faster and faster. The wolf turned back toward the others. Little Turtle ran faster, yelling, jumping, and swinging the bow around over his head like a crazy person. He raised the bow and slapped the hind end of the lone wolf. It yelped in surprise, and with tail between legs, sped through the pack and beyond. Now the pack spread out left and right, trying to avoid the swinging bow. Little Turtle shouted and charged among them, like a fierce, crazed beast, and the wolves decided they did not want any part of him. They regrouped down the slope and turned away to scout the buffalo herd again.

White Crow smiled from his hiding place behind the distant rocks. He stood, nodding appreciatively, and started home. He had been following Little Turtle. When the boy returned to the tribe, he would start calling him Fears Not Wolf or perhaps He Who Chases Wolf. He would tell the story of this encounter at the evening fire; a story he knew the People would love. Because fearlessness in the face of insurmountable odds made the best stories. If Little Turtle was not afraid of a whole wolf pack, he would become a champion warrior and later a chief.

Little Turtle walked back up the hill to retrieve his blanket and bag. He smiled to himself. The encounter with the wolves had been incredibly scary and intensely fun. No wonder men wanted to be warriors. No wonder young boys wanted to be men.

He wrapped his blanket around his shoulders and watched the wolf pack trot northwest. The rising sun warmed his body. The meadowlark called. The quail's warbling song carried up the hill from the stream bed, and he smiled contentedly. A red fox came out of its den and watched the buffalo herd and watched the boy. And it watched the jack rabbit intently. But the fox retreated back into the den as the human began walking across the prairie toward the distant mountains.

The river ran wide with snowmelt but not yet raging. Little Turtle was not worried about the cold water, but he did not know how to swim. He worked his way up the mountain, looking for a way to cross the river. He knew that if he went far enough, the river would become a stream he could step across easily. At the higher elevations it was still winter and the nights were bitter cold. But with his shelter out of the wind and a small fire, the weather didn't bother him too much.

He had planned to climb higher up the mountain, but then came upon the downed tree. A great pine straddled the wide stream, ten feet above the water. Although covered in over a foot of snow, he was confident in his ability to navigate the natural bridge. How dangerous could it be? He was an accomplished warrior, who could pass any test with audacity.

The root ball stood twenty feet high, and he climbed up and over the roots to get to the trunk. He smiled. He had walked over narrow logs before without a problem. This big tree was almost like walking on flat ground. He stepped off confidently but slowly. With each step he was rewarded with a sense of accomplishment. He could already imagine himself on the other side. Another victory. When he told the story around the fire, the tree would be only six inches wide and one hundred feet above the raging river, wobbling in the high winds tearing down the river canyon. He chuckled at his mythical prowess. Shouts At The Wind would laugh and jump up and down.

One second he was walking confidently across the log, and the next he was falling. He did not realize that a big chunk of the tree had been torn out in the fall, disguised by the thick, smooth layer of snow. His foot shot through the soft powder, and he was in the water before he could think.

For a stream only thirty feet wide, it was deep at that spot. He called out in surprise then went under, flailing. For a moment he surfaced, then he was under again, turned and twisted by the fast-moving water. Panic shot through him. Nothing he did worked. He pounded the water with his hands and kicked wildly with his feet, but he felt Death's icy fingers probing for his heart and mind.

In his head he heard White Crow's calm and distant counsel, "Don't panic."

Was White Crow here? Why wasn't he helping him? He went down again, trying to hold his breath. How was he supposed to relax, when he was fighting to survive and on the verge of drowning?

But the message resonated. His lungs burned with the effort to not suck in the cold water, which he knew would bring an instant end to his short life. He forced himself to relax and stop fighting. As a sense of calm came upon him, he opened his eyes. He could see. Although the water was frothy, it was crystal clear, and he saw the large boulder approaching. If he couldn't swim, maybe he could crawl out of the water, like the turtle he was named after.

He slammed into the boulder, which had also caught an assortment of branches. The first branch slipped out of his right hand. He desperately grabbed another with his left and held on, trying to pull himself upward. He was on the left side of the boulder, fighting the current. His head just broke the surface enough to inhale a great draft of air. Then his grip slipped away, and the river tumbled and tossed him again.

His world began to fade, and he knew his quest had ended. His eyes were open, but all he saw was water swirling around. What would Shouts At The Wind say? What would his uncle think? He had failed and they would never know.

He noticed that the gravel bed of the stream was getting closer, but it didn't mean anything to him. Something grabbed his coat, and he saw moccasin feet in the water, standing in the gravel. What did that mean?

When he woke up, he was shivering uncontrollably, leaning against a boulder, wrapped in blankets in front of a large fire. His teeth chattered uncontrollably.

"Ah, there ya be, youngin'," a kindly voice said.

He was so cold and miserable he could not even move his eyes. He just stared at the fire, then noticed his cloths hanging from various sticks on the other side, steam rising steadily.

"Thought ya was a fish, heh?" The man's voice broke into a chortling laugh. "Fortunate fur you, the trail runs along the stream right about there. Saw ya fall off that big log up yonder and got out on the sandbar in a hurry ta catch ya goin' by, sort a scoopin' ya up."

Little Turtle finally noticed the mountain man on the left side of the fire, stirring something in a frying pan. He liked the smell. The mountain man was dressed like an Indian: leather leggings and knee-high moccasins, long buffalo coat, and beaver hat with beaver head prominently displayed up front. The hair on his head and face was white and long, but his eyebrows were like fat black caterpillars. His front teeth were missing and

24

the top of his right ear. A prominent knife hung on his right side and another inside the top of his right moccasin. Although he had a care-worn appearance with skin of brown leather, typical of many mountain men, he had a ready smile and a twinkle in his eye, like he knew a funny secret.

"Onst this here elk stew's hot and bubbly, we'll get some of it in ya, then you'll be right as rain."

Ever so slowly, Little Turtle's chattering teeth slowed down and stopped beating his face. He pulled his hands out of the blankets and put them before the fire.

"Looky here, boy. Take this," the man said, handing him a tin cup. "Good. That's it. Hold the handle. Good."

Little Turtle took the cup and held it with both trembling hands.

"Last a the coffee, that there is," the man said wistfully. "Put a might a sugar in it. You'll like that, if I'm any kinda judge." He poured himself a cup and sat back against the stump. "Lucky fur you, I got caught up in the high country this year. Just worked ma way through the pass yesterday, now as the snow's finally meltin'."

Little Turtle did not understand a word the man was saying. Over the years he had seen five mountain men. They usually traded for furs, or hides, and almost always asked where the People found their yellow jewelry. In sign language, he said he did not understand.

The man nodded. "Well, child, don't ya worry none 'bout that. I'm a chatty sort a feller, I guess from livin' alone sa long. Why I'd just as soon talk ta ma mule, as a person." He chuckled again.

Little Turtle liked the black drink. He had had honey before, but this tasted different. Between the warm drink and the fire, he slowly stopped shaking.

"Now, put your feet out there, too," the man said. He took off his moccasins and put his big feet before the fire, pointing at Little Turtle to do the same. "That's the way, boy."

The man sniffed the stew carefully. "She's right done!" He gave the contents one more swirl with the wooden spoon, then heaped the lumpy brown concoction onto a pie tin plate. "Mountain lion I shot two days ago, wild onions, salt from the slick over in Dorado, four old, soft sproutin' potatoes, and the last of the old carrots. Would'a had dried mushrooms, but ya come a week late."

Little Turtle began eating with his hands, carefully pulling out chunks of meat. Although too hot to hold, he managed to get pieces into his mouth, chewing gratefully.

The mountain man smiled to see it, eating his food with the wooden spoon. "Sorry boy, only spoon I got. Ya probably don't know 'bout spoons anyways."

Little Turtle wolfed down the stew, and the kind man quickly refilled the plate. The second plate was soon gone, and the boy realized he felt mostly normal.

The mountain man licked his tin clean and sat back. He had eaten only one helping of stew. "Too bad we don't have any corn bread or somethin' to wipe up the juice with. I miss bread and things made with flour. When I get ta Denver, I'm tellin' ya, first thing I'm gettin' is an apple pie. Haven't had fruit for nigh on four months. Missin' fruit somethin' terrible."

Little Turtle copied the mountain man and wiped his plate clean with his tongue.

The man took the plate and began wiping it out with snow. "I ain't never run outta food, but one year I run outta coffee and like ta died, yes siree, liked ta died. Ain't partial ta tea, not even a little. Now, I bring extry coffee, which is why I got some now. I don't mind runnin' low on food, on occasion, long's I got coffee. I know it's odd, but well, guess I'm odd. Mother Nature will supply most anythin' ya need up in these here hills, but she's stingy 'bout her coffee, and I'm not partial to substitutes."

Little Turtle stared at the fire, listening to the man talk, and his eyes slowly closed.

"Now you take that coffee there. Why I've boiled those grounds two maybe three times. Some folks just toss'm out after one use, but when you're traipsin' 'round wild country ya gotta make things last—stretch'm outta little."

He looked at the boy, chin on chest, and smiled. He gently laid him down and tucked in the blankets. He pulled on his moccasins and stood. In a few minutes, he packed his cooking gear on the mule and left the boy sleeping by the fire.

When Little Turtle awoke, he wondered if he had been in a vision dream. He stood and dressed in the hot clothes, wondering about the mountain man. Was it a dream? No, a trail in the snow led down the mountain. He could see over a mile, but there was no sign of the man. He must have slept for a long time. He felt thankful to find his bow, quiver and bag laid by the stump. The sun was just setting, so he gathered more wood for the night, thankful that the man had left him an extra blanket.

Over seven days, Little Turtle wandered down the western side of the mountain range—what became known as the Sangre de Cristos—without finding any bear sign. Perhaps Great Bear lingered in his winter den, he thought. He started back up through the foothills, more on the east side, never in a hurry. He walked slowly, listening, sniffing the air, studying the ground for signs. The old men said a bear smells oily. He was not sure what they meant, but he hoped for an unusual smell, something distinct and different.

CHAPTER THREE

T he great bears, closely related to the long-legged North American giant short-faced bear— Arctodus simus—ruled the land for hundreds of thousands of years, since what is called the Pleistocene Era—2.6 million to 11,700 years ago. They were the top predators, and they knew it. They feared no creature. They watched the last dinosaurs fade from memory, buried under ash and mud in what became Saskatchewan, Montana, Wyoming and Colorado. They watched the great walls of ice creep down from the north, retreating and advancing, over and over again, for tens of thousands of years.

The saber-tooth tigers, American cheetahs and lions, and the dire wolf avoided the great bears. The woolly mammoth, mastodon, giant beaver, and giant sloth did not fear them, although they knew that situation could change in an unwary moment. Although a full-grown male great bear topped out at over three thousand pounds, they were content to graze on grasses, munch various leaves, insects and seasonal fruit. They loved to sniff out tubers and dig up whole acres of ground to get vegetables like wild potatoes and onions.

But once a year, just before hibernation, their body told them something extra was needed. Their high-fat food of choice was the giant ground sloth. One ground sloth could feed four or five bears, and they would go to their prepared dens and lay down for the long sleep.

Their smaller cousin, the cave bear, once ranged across Europe and Asia. In the modern age, their closest, and slightly smaller relative is the Kodiak bear—a type of grizzly, of Kodiak Island, off the west coast of Alaska. A full-grown Kodiak boar has a pawprint up to eighteen inches long and often stands five feet at the shoulders when standing on four feet. Kodiaks and polar bears can reach a height of ten feet. A captive Kodiak bear attained the weight of 2,400 pounds with nine inches of fat.

But the great bears had a footprint over twenty inches long with eight-inch claws well beyond that. At the end of winter, after a long sleep in the den, Great Bear weighed a lean two thousand, seven hundred pounds and stood sixteen feet tall on his hind feet.

After the comet slammed into North America near present-day Chicago—twelve thousand years ago, cold and darkness settled on the land in what scientists call the Quaternary Extinction. The trees and grasses failed and most of the animals, like the mammoth, mastodon, and giant sloth, starved and died off during the following year. In short order, the large predators that relied on them for food—the saber-tooth tiger, dire wolf, and American lion—soon followed. A few predators, who had been living in the far south or the far north, survived, barely.

By the time the land recovered, it was too late for many. Into this crisis came the first humans. With most of the big predators gone, those large grazing animals that had found a way to survive the catastrophe were easily killed off, the giant sloth among them. Over time, the great bears did not put on enough fat before the harsh winters, and more and more of them did not wake up in the spring. After ruling the continent for over one hundred thousand years as the undisputed top predator, only one remained.

When the first humans braved the icy passage across the northern sea to enter North America, the great bears were already ancient. Like the many creatures before them, those first humans also gave way to the great bears, respecting and referring to them as a big brother, a wise ancestor, embodying the guiding principles of survival and harmonious living with the world. Village Shaman's called on the Spirit of Great Bear to guide them in choices, bring the buffalo when needed, protect the People from times of tribulation, starvation, and defeat from enemies. In some clans, the Shaman called upon Great Bear to punish offenders of rules governing animal and human society. As the most noble of the Great Spirit's creatures, the magnificent bear was not seen strictly as an animal, but as a deity whose beneficence could be called upon and expected. Interestingly, some clans described a great bear that ate humans and stood as tall as elephants. In our modern times, people exploring the far northern reaches of Canada have reported seeing a monster brown bear, larger than any grizzly in existence.

Great Bear of the Sangre de Cristo Mountains did not have a formal name. Over the years, the occasional Indian or mountain man or miner just called him, *"That big damn grizzly!"* Although he looked like a big grizzly—and could be accurately described as a first cousin, he had an almost blonde sheen to his deep brown coat when the morning or afternoon sun hit it on an angle. Like the largest grizzlies, he had a mantel of blond-white hair across his shoulders, that ran down to his elbows and up to his ears, and along the back to his tail. This was not a sign of old age, but common among great bears in their prime.

Life was basic and uncomplicated: his days simple. When the berries were plentiful, he lingered in the blackberry groves. He dug up tubers and mushrooms, and tore into beehives to get the rich, delicious honey. Just before hibernation, he craved fatty meat. In his ancestral mind, he somehow understood that his favorite or preferred meal was no longer available. Salmon alone did not quite satisfy him, although he ate enough for ten grizzlies. So he took the first big creature that crossed his path—usually an old moose or elk. His family had been one of the few to transition from eating giant sloth before winter, but it was never quite enough. Fewer and fewer of the great bears awoke in the spring.

Great Bear wondered that he could not find a mate. Part of him yearned for a mate, causing him to stand on the high ridge for hours, sniffing the wind currents. No scent captured his attention or roused his passion. He could not understand the wistful sense of change and loss, the melancholy of despair and extinction. He did not feel sad. He only knew, deep down, that something was wrong. He did not realize that he was the last of his kind.

On Little Turtle's first walk through the mountains, he didn't find anything. He established a primitive camp near the southern tip of the mountain range. The next day he killed a deer, dressed it out, and hung the strips of meat to dry. Over a one-week period, he worked his way up the eastern side of the mountain range then came back down the western side, what the elders described as Great Bear territory. Still, he didn't find any tracks or signs. Sitting alone under his lean-to, he made a vow to not give up until the first snows came the following winter. Then he would assume Great Bear had either moved on or had died.

As the sun cleared the tree tops, he sat before his small, smokeless fire and studied the river in the distance. On his next scouting of the area, he would work deeper into the woods, to see if he could find Great Bear's den—at least the elders said bears lived in caves. If the dead body was there, he would remove the front claws and head back to the village. If the bear was not there, he was not sure how to proceed. He had not found tracks, so he would have to assume it moved into the higher mountains in the north. Again, he would not relent until the first snows. He hated the idea of admitting defeat, but if the bear no longer lived, it was not really a personal failure. He would try his best and that would be sufficient. When he went back to the village, he could still hold up his head without shame.

He worked his way along the river valley on the west side of the mountains, near the wide bank, through piles of river-tossed trees and boulders. The sun's warming rays heated the land, causing smells to rise. He froze in place, nose lifted, sniffing. A faint scent flitted through the morning air, elusive. Something *different*. It seemed to have an oily texture to it, or was that his imagination? His heart beat faster. The soft breeze flowed down the mountain side on his right—the east. Probably winds from the prairie beyond, he thought, warmed by the rising sun, coursing over the peaks and ridges and down this side.

In his search, he had seen three grizzlies and did not want to surprise them: one, an old silverback brute, busy demolishing a rotten log for grubs. That big bear smelled like wet dog. This odor was different. Maybe it was not a bear. He carefully worked his way to the right, up the steep slope. He found a well-used game trail and followed it.

Half way up the mountain, beside the trail, he found a large bear scat, bigger than any he had ever seen, already drawing flies. He touched the pile. Still warm. He couldn't help smiling. Less than an hour old, he thought. He studied the ground. No tracks. How could there be no tracks? Could the bear somehow keep its claws from digging in? Wait. There. A tuft of course golden-brown hair pulled out by the wild rose thorns. He rolled the long hairs in his fingers and brought the wad up to his nose. Grizzly hide came to mind with something else, maybe that oily smell the elders described. Great Bear must be close. He felt a thrill of fear and quickly strung his bow.

He peeled bark off a birch tree and fashioned a crude box to hold a little of the bear scat. He didn't know exactly why he wanted it, but there might be a use, perhaps as a lure or to mask his own odor.

Little Turtle slowly followed the trail up the mountain, stopping often to listen and sniff. He thought he should have seen the bear by now, unless it had noticed him and run off. But the wind was still in his favor, in his face. He stopped on the ridge crest. A woodpecker drilled continuously on a nearby tree. In the clear blue sky, he could see far out onto the plains to the east. A herd of buffalo grazed in the far distance: a black smudge of dots on the distant white-green grass. I will never tire of this view, he thought. He studied the east ridge and forest down below his feet. Nothing. Where had the bear gone? Why are there no tracks? he wondered again.

The wind swirled and his nose caught an imperceptible *something,* briefly. The hairs on the back of his neck rose involuntarily, and he shuddered. Great Bear was near; he just knew it. Felt it. Very near. Probably watching him. He turned slowly, looking all around. Nothing. But there had to be something. The wind freshened, still coming from the east, swirling occasionally, as wind often does. Maybe Great Bear is down the east ridge there. He started down the hill, not exactly sure what he would do when he found the bear. He smiled to think that he would shoot an arrow and run like crazy.

Great Bear knew something was following him. He had been around long enough to know who should be in the mountains and who was a stranger. From the bluff he had watched the creature sneak through the forest below. He lay with his head on his wide paws—the paws hanging over the steep cliff—just watching. He was curious about the stranger, but did not want to invite a confrontation. He desired to be left alone. At times, he watched. At other times, he followed quietly. For Great Bear, one of the most intelligent creatures to ever walk the land, it became something of a game, a change in his predictable and normal routine. He was having fun. He often walked to the side of established trails—foliage permitting, so he left little evidence of his passing. Unlike some bears, usually, his claws only dug in when attacking, or if the ground was uneven or soft and wet.

On that early spring morning, he wandered down to the river and drank deeply, then lay in the water. The icy water felt good. He drank again then caught and ate seven salmon. Late in the morning, he started back up the mountain. Through the trees he saw the stranger, walking up the river valley. He quickly moved up the hill until about half way, then squatted by the trail side to poop—something he never did near a main trail— then deliberately brushed the other side of the trail where the wild roses grew, knowing a tuft of hair would remain. This was fun. Near the top, he pulled off to the left side, carefully picking his way over the rock slide until he could lay down in the copse of ancient weather-beaten pine trees. From that vantage point, peering through the thick limbs, he could see who followed without being seen.

Little Turtle quietly crept down the mountain to the main trail on the east side and followed it south to his little camp. Nothing. But he knew he had been close. Very close.

He sat on the gray log and absently chewed jerky, thinking about the walk that day. Down in the valley by the river, he had worked through rough terrain, slowly moving north. His nose sensed something, so he had followed the trail up the mountain. Then he found the scat and tuft of hair. As he thought about the experience, he absently twirled the long hairs between his fingers. From there, he climbed the steep slope up to the ridge. Great Bear must have been close, because he sensed it: maybe a combination of smells, indistinct sounds, or unconsciously seeing something that did not quite register. On the far side of the ridge, he found nothing— only at the top. When he stood on the ridge, he had sensed the bear's nearness.

He thought back. What was there? A wide clear space. Scattered individual weathered trees. A burned

41

out, lightning struck tree. A rockslide. Off to the left beyond the rockslide, just down the ridge on the west side, a small group of trees. He tried to remember every detail. If Great Bear was close, sensed but not seen…he caught his breath. The bear could have been in no other place. He must have been in those trees. Had to be.

As he pondered this new idea, a frown and lines of concern became deeply etched on his young face. He looked out at the river and stopped chewing. Great Bear knew he was standing there. Was it possible that Great Bear had lured him to that spot? He shuddered to think that Great Bear had been *behind* him. Great Bear could have attacked, and he would not have seen the bear charging until too late. He realized this was not like hunting other grizzlies. Little Turtle felt like the wounded rabbit the bobcat played with before killing and eating it.

Part of him was aware of a deep and persistent warning, clanging in his mind. A smart man would flee this area and this unusual bear, who seemed to be toying with him. But he was young, fearless, and could not accept the idea that an animal of any kind was that smart, or able to outwit a mighty Cheyenne hunter, as he saw himself. How could he sit around the evening fire and tell the story of his visionary hunt? He would stand proudly, beat his chest, and say: On the last day, Great Bear scared me to death, so I ran home as fast as I could. Then the tribe would certainly give him a new name: Runs from Bear, or Fearful Squirrel, or One Wing Crow.

He stood, shaking himself, then ran over to the river and threw himself in. The bitter cold water shocked his body, but he splashed it all over and finally lay down on his back on the smooth rocks near the shore, submerged to his face. He would conquer his fears like he conquered the cold water. He would take control of his body and his fear, and he would succeed where lesser warriors quaked and slunk away.

He sat up in the water, teeth chattering. Well, two could play at this game, he reasoned. If Great Bear could play with him, he would play with Great Bear.

Early the next morning, he broke camp and walked south, around the tip of the mountain range, then north along the east slope. He wanted to find Great Bear's den. He followed a well-defined trail and took every side trail he could find, leading up the hill or down. He knew it would take time and persistence, both of which he had in abundance. When he found nothing along a side trail, he went back to the main trail and continued. On the eighth day, he followed a vague trail wandering up the slope through thick brush and trees. After working around an outcropping of rocks and several ancient fallen trees, he spotted a cave.

"There you are," he whispered quietly to himself.

He approached cautiously, fearfully looking all around. Just as he was about to enter, he hesitated. Instead, he climbed up the side of the hill and settled in among the ferns, just above the cave entrance. He rubbed wet dirt over his face and body. Then he had an idea, and reached inside the birch bark box he had made and rubbed some of the Great Bear scat all over his body. If he could mask his own scent, he might become invisible to the beast. And if this was the bear's cave, then he would tease the poor creature mercilessly. The People would laugh at his story. Too bad he did not have any witnesses.

Just before dark, he heard the whisper of something coming. His heart quickened. A great hulking shape walked around the outcropping and onto the ledge in front of the cave. Little Turtle caught his breath. The bear had approached more quietly than he thought possible. He did not realize how incredibly huge the bear was: twice the size of the old, silver-backed boar he had seen down by the river. This bear was taller at the shoulders than he was tall.

Suddenly, it stood, facing down the mountain. Little Turtle fearfully lowered his head into the detritus of the forest, trying to become invisible, because if the bear turned around, it would be looking straight at him. He held his breath. He could hear the bear panting and sniffing. It did turn to face him. He could tell the massive creature was looking and sniffing in his direction. Had he fooled it? Or would the bear reach out in a moment and pull him off the slope, to be torn to shreds?

The bear noises stopped. Little Turtle tentatively lifted his head and peeked through the ferns. The bear was gone, probably into the cave. He smiled. Now I know where you live, he thought.

When he got back to his camp, he started a fire and could not stop grinning. In the morning, he gathered up his things and started searching for a place to camp closer to the cave. But not too close. Just closer. If he was going to play with the bear, he did not want to travel so far each day.

CHAPTER FOUR

Black Spotted Horse watched as Little Turtle approached along the trail, but he waited until he had walked by to jump out and scare him. As expected, and hoped for, Little Turtle cried out.

"You should not do that!" Little Turtle shouted angrily.

"What? Are you not happy to see me?" Black Spotted Horse asked, hands arrogantly on hips.

After his initial fright, Little Turtle had to smile. "I *am* glad to see you." He leaned forward and punched Black Spotted Horse's right shoulder—hard.

"I have been looking for you," Black Spotted Horse admitted, rubbing his shoulder.

Little Turtle looked at him quizzically. "Why?"

"What do you mean, why? Because you have been gone for a long time and no one knew what happened to you." He did not tell him that White Crow told everyone about the wolf pack encounter, so he figured what direction Little Turtle had taken.

Little Turtle shrugged. Although he was glad to see his friend, he wished he had not come looking for him.

This quest was personal, and he did not want to share the adventure or the growing story. "You should go," he said dismissively with the wave of a hand, and turned away.

"Go? What are you doing?" Black Spotted Horse persisted.

Little Turtle looked all around the forest. "Today, I am moving from one camp to another." He paused, thinking. "Well, come with me."

"Wait. My horse is down the hill there."

As time passed, Black Spotted Horse wondered what became of Little Turtle. The adults assured him that his young friend would eventually return, most likely a wiser man for the experience.

"Wiser how?" Black Spotted Horse had asked. The idea that Little Turtle could become wiser than him grated on his mind.

White Crow replied, "You learn things about yourself when alone, when on vision quest."

Like many boys, he found the answer cryptic and vague. One of those things you cannot really know about until you do it. Like, how do you feel after killing your first enemy? People felt different things, so it was different for each person. No single answer worked for everyone.

After half a day, Little Turtle found a place that seemed likely for a camp: a dense group of trees. In the center was a little open and flat area not more than twenty feet round. He rolled two large stones from the center to the perimeter. A tree had fallen half way, so that it leaned against other trees at a shallow angle. He would stack limbs against that tree to create a lean-to, and if the bear came around, he could run up the leaning tree, like a squirrel to get away. Easy. Fun.

He started a fire and explained to Black Spotted Horse all that had transpired with Great Bear.

"You must be very brave or very foolish," his friend said seriously. He pushed a stick deeper into the fire. "I am not sure which, yet." But he thought foolish more likely.

This irritated Little Turtle. "I did not invite you here, and yet you judge me."

Black Spotted Horse gave him a lopsided smirk. "White Crow told a story around the fire." He paused. "How you drove off a pack of wolves by swinging your bow and slapping them with it."

Little Turtle grinned, remembering that cold morning, which seemed so long ago now.

"Is it true?"

"Yes. They surprised me." He looked at his friend. "I was just lucky." He was happy about the story, but distressed that he did not know White Crow had followed him.

"Not the way your uncle tells it. He made you sound like the new chief and the greatest warrior of the tribe." In the sharing of this story with Little Turtle, Black Spotted Horse realized that jealousy had driven him to search out his friend. He had always imagined himself—the chief's only son—as the greatest warrior and future chief of the tribe. His search for Little Turtle was to find out if the story was true. Black Spotted Horse jumped up, hands on hips, his usual pose. "A pack of wolves? Or was it actually only one old, gray, toothless lobo?"

Little Turtle bristled at the accusation. "Do you think my uncle lied, or that I did not fight off the wolves as he said in the story?"

"I think the story gets better and the wolf gets bigger each time it is told."

Little Turtle's neck and ears flushed red with anger. He started to stand then fell back laughing. At first only a chuckle, staring up at Black Spotted Horse, but then a strong and steady belly laugh. Even Black Spotted Horse had to grin and then laugh. He plopped back down.

"Tomorrow you will see why I am still here." Little Turtle grinned wickedly. "Ayee, and you will know my uncle's story is true. If I told you Great Bear was big—the biggest bear in the world—you would scoff and call me a liar to my face. But wait until you see him. Then you will know fear like never before."

Black Spotted Horse fell silent, studying his friend. Little Turtle's eyes were grave and serious; and in his heart, he knew his friend spoke the truth. Although his jealousy lingered, his respect grew.

The next day they crept stealthily toward the cave, keeping the north wind in their faces. They carefully moved to the ledge in front of the cave and peered in. The cave was deep and dark. Little Turtle could not tell if Great Bear was home or not. He boldly walked up to the cave entrance, squatted down and pooped, then ran off, laughing. He was still a kid, after all. Whether the bear was in the cave or not, this *gift* was sure to get a reaction. Same kind of gift he left me, Little Turtle reasoned. He ran up the hill until he could just see the cave and stopped behind a wide tree.

Black Spotted Horse caught up with him, slightly winded. He was a horseman, not used to running up mountains. "What did you just do?"

"Great Bear left me a gift like that, and so I left him one."

"But he is Great Bear."

"So. We are playing a game," Little Turtle said indignantly. "Play along or go home."

Black Spotted Horse frowned but sat down next to Little Turtle to watch the cave.

Three hours later, Great Bear approached from the north and walked up to the cave entrance.

Black Spotted Horse whispered in awe, "Ayee, his size! You did not lie. He is truly *the* Great Bear Spirit."

At the cave entrance, the large head lowered, and Little Turtle knew Great Bear was inspecting the gift. The bear stood on his hind legs, sniffing all around. A thrill of fear ran through Little Turtle before he realized the wind was off his right shoulder, from the east now. Still, he hunched down more. The bear looked all around then turned toward the cave and roared.

Why did he roar? Little Turtle wondered. Did I make him mad? It might be time to retreat to the new camp. He motioned to Black Spotted Horse and backed away until out of sight of the cave, and ran deep into the forest.

The next morning before first light, Little Turtle woke Black Spotted Horse. They eased out of the little camp and cautiously wound through the trees and up to the ridge. As the sky lightened, Little Turtle found where two trails came up from the east side and crossed over to the west side. Despite the lack of defined tracks, he figured these were the two main trails Great Bear used to go to water. Again, with a wide grin, he peed into the middle of and all around each trail. This was fun, sure to drive Great Bear crazy. He did not need to watch the bear's reaction. Instead, he ran north along the ridge for several miles, then down the west side and across the river. Black Spotted Horse followed quietly.

An hour later they heard a loud and persistent roar from up the mountain. Black Spotted Horse stood, arms folded across his chest, face stern. "Did you ever wonder if Great Bear thinks of your pee as a territorial mark—a sign of dominance or invasion?"

Little Turtle lay on a large warm rock. "Are you telling me what to do?" he asked testily, his right eyebrow rising.

Black Spotted Horse slowly shook his head in dismay. "Perhaps Great Bear will feel threatened and the need to move. This action of yours might even anger him into fighting. The game will be over, and you will be dead before you realize it was not a game to Great Bear." And he would probably be dead along with his friend.

Little Turtle stood, facing his friend, his fists tight at his sides, jaw muscles flexing in and out. After a full minute, he saw the wisdom of the comment and relaxed. His tense shoulders slumped. "You might be right," he admitted, turning away. He stared into the sparkling river water, trying to determine what his true motivation had been. "But if the bear is on this side of the ridge, then maybe we should visit the cave again. I want to leave him one more gift."

The afternoon sun gave way to dark, threatening clouds, a cold wind coming off the snow-covered mountains in the north. At the cave, they waited and listened. It seemed safe. Little Turtle's previous poop was gone, which didn't surprise him. He crept into the cave and peed all over where the bear slept. He ran out of the cave, laughing. Black Spotted Horse ran after him, shaking his head sadly. The heavy rain began to fall, and they ran all the way back to their little camp.

The copse of trees was too tight for his horse, so Black Spotted Horse had been staking it further down the hill where the grass was fresh and thick. The temperature dropped. The boys added branches and moss to the little lean-to to keep out the rain and lit a small fire. Off in the distance, they heard Great Bear roar.

Little Turtle smiled at first, chuckling to himself, then frowned. He stared into the small fire, deep in thought. "I wonder how angry the bear is now?" He felt an unease in his soul, as if he had gone a little too far with this silly game. It would be dark soon. He looked off toward the cave. Could the bear track them here in the growing rain?

Black Spotted Horse sipped from the U.S. Cavalry canteen he always carried. "I can see you are not afraid of Great Bear and tease him mercilessly." He hesitated and finally sighed. "So White Crow's story about the wolves must be true."

Little Turtle looked up and smiled at him. For a long time, he sat with his hands before the flames, adding little twigs and sticks and pinecones when needed. "It is true; I have enjoyed my time with Great Bear, but maybe we should go. Great Bear seems more like a brother to me now. I would never torment an elder of the tribe like this." He took a deep breath. "And yet…and yet, that is exactly what I have been doing."

He looked up, studying Black Spotted Horse who remained passive, not showing any emotion. "The young men will laugh when they hear about my gifts to Great Bear, but the Shaman—he will be displeased." After a long pause, "My uncle, White Crow, will be displeased." He shook his head sadly. "My actions have *not* been the actions of a great warrior." As he considered this line of thinking, he felt shame fill his heart. He added a stick to the fire, frowning.

He looked up at Black Spotted Horse, wiping a lone tear from his eye. "We will go home in the morning."

The bear roared and the boys cried out.

When Great Bear found the human scat in front of his cave, he felt anger for the first time in his long life. It was an emotion he had never had to feel. The scat he left along the trail was one thing, but leaving it in front of his home was something different. It was a violation. A threat. He roared and violently swiped the scat off the ledge and down the mountain.

Where was the creature? Did it want to fight him? Take the only home he had ever known?

The next day Great Bear walked up to the ridge, heading for water. On top of the ridge, in the middle of the trail, the creature had left its mark. He felt his territory threatened, shrinking, his world closing in. He would have to leave these mountains forever or eliminate the creature. He did not feel like moving. He stood and roared in frustration.

In his anger, he followed the creature's scent down to the river then lost it. He roared again and splashed the water angrily. Two salmon flew up onto the bank, so he ate them, temporarily forgetting about the problem.

Great Bear lingered at the river, catching a few early season salmon. The sky clouded and turned black, so he started back to the cave.

As he approached, he knew something was wrong. The creature's scent was strong, very strong. He stood, sniffing, looking up and down the hill. When satisfied that the creature was not lurking outside the cave, he entered. The creature's scent overpowered his nose and mind. He dropped to all fours and charged. Nothing. He stopped, sniffing the cave floor. His anger blazed. His home had been defiled. The creature wanted him to leave his land, and it wanted to take over his home. The creature was forcing him out. His eyes narrowed. He stepped onto the ledge and roared, foam and spittle flying. They would fight! He would drive off the invader! The cold rain intensified, but he put his nose to the ground and started south.

The heavy rain pounded but the wind swirled and shifted, and Great Bear caught the faint scent of wood smoke. His head lowered and his eyes blazed in unabated anger. The forest grew thicker but he followed the thin, wandering trail in the air. He circled the dense copse of trees, looking for a likely way in. He always stepped quietly, but the heavy rain also masked any sound, making the forest floor soft and squishy. He nudged through a narrow opening by a large boulder. He spied the flicker of light off a limb and roared, pushing through the narrow gap between two trees, while swiping at smaller trees with his claws to enlarge the opening.

Little Turtle and Black Spotted Horse screamed involuntarily. Chunks of bark flew through the air. Great Bear was so close, they could smell the lingering, foul smell of salmon on his breath. Little Turtle grabbed his bow and quiver and ran up the leaning tree, as planned. He wished now he had practiced the maneuver: difficult in the daylight, now treacherous in the flickering light of his little fire.

"Climb higher!" he shouted at Black Spotted Horse.

Black Spotted Horse had a bow also, but left it and his knife by the fire as he followed Little Turtle up the slanting tree in sheer panic.

Great Bear bent two small trees out of the way to get into the open area and attacked the leaning tree. The tree shook. The bear stood, staring up at the boys and roared.

Black Spotted Horse covered his ears. "Climb higher!" he shouted, since he was lower on the tree and closer to the angry bear.

They moved from the slanting tree into the tall pine and kept climbing. Soon they were over twice as high as Great Bear could reach.

"Maybe he will get tired of this and go home," Black Spotted Horse said hopefully. He was already shivering with cold.

What Great Bear did next startled them.

Great Bear immediately understood how the creatures made it into the big tree so easily, so he pushed against the leaning tree and toppled it over. The ground shuddered as the eighty-foot spruce crashed to the ground. He roared, studying his prey. If one tree could come down, so could the other. He swiped at the tree base repeatedly, a spot eight feet off the ground, bark flying. He did not tire. He swiped and bit into the soft inner bark. The bear suddenly lunged at the tree, and it groaned at the impact. The fire grew larger as pieces of dry bark landed among the flames.

Little Turtle looked around, wondering if they could jump like squirrels to another tree. Maybe. Their tree shook again. I could die here, he realized. He thought he had only one option and dying was not it. He was wet and shook involuntarily with cold. How could a simple arrow kill such a large beast? Perhaps, the arrow would kill Great Bear if perfectly placed into the skull. No creature could take an arrow to the head and survive. The tree shook and groaned, then emitted a loud crack. It began to lean. Little Turtle made his decision. He sat out on a limb, legs on both sides, and nocked an arrow.

Black Spotted Horse looked up at him and became alarmed. "You may have the strongest bow in the tribe, but an arrow will not kill Great Bear!" he shouted. "No arrow can kill him!"

"We will see." He drew the gut string back to his right ear. It was a powerful bow, the hardest to pull in the tribe. His arrowheads were long, and finely crafted works of deadly art. Little Turtle was confident of the arrow's ability to kill the bear, and his skill to place the arrowhead precisely where needed. And besides, didn't he come here to kill Great Bear?

"Do not shoot!"

He let loose the arrow.

The arrow struck Great Bear between the left eye and left ear, penetrating the thick skull. But the skull of a great bear is over one-inch thick. The shot was accurate, powerful, and perfectly placed. The exquisite arrowhead held its shape; it even split the skull in that area. And the two-inch long, flint arrowhead penetrated half its length into the brain.

But it was not a killing blow.

Great Bear cried out in pain and surprise, and fell back. A searing, blinding, agony burned through his head and body, never experienced before. The huge arms thrashed and swiped at the offending object, breaking off the arrow shaft. But the long, pointed flint arrowhead remained buried in his brain. The left eye pain was blindingly intense, and the bear winced and staggered, shaking his shaggy head.

As the shock of the arrow impact began to wear off, an incomprehensible fury rose up in his chest, and Great Bear roared louder than ever before. It was a thunderous explosion of surprise, frustration, but especially madness. He rose on his two hind feet and noticed the puny creatures, as if for the first time, fearfully climbing higher into the tree. The surprise and frustration of the attack melted away so that only madness remained. Madness settled deep into his heart.

Where a moment before he had been about to abandon the tree and the fugitives, now the bear tore into it with renewed strength and anger. The tree leaned more. Little Turtle fitted another arrow. Just as he let it loose, the tree shook and the arrow grazed the skin of the bear's left shoulder. The boys scrambled upward.

Little Turtle shouted, "Climb higher! If we get high enough, maybe we can leap into that other tree when this one falls."

"Black Spotted Horse wept as he slowly reached for the flimsy upper limbs. His hands were so cold, he had difficulty holding on, and up in the tree top, it was too dark to see clearly.

Great Bear savagely threw his immense weight into the trunk. The tree cracked mournfully and began a slow fall.

Little Turtle threw his bow and quiver away, preparing to grab a limb on the next tree with both hands. He reached out, but the falling tree rotated. He successfully grabbed a limb with his left hand, but limbs from the falling tree slapped his face and body, pulling his grip away. He fell, bouncing from limb to limb; his scream cut off suddenly as he slammed into the ground from almost fifty feet in the air. The moss-covered floor of the forest partially broke his fall. He rolled to his feet and ran blindly into the dark, holding his right side and three broken ribs.

As the tree fell, Black Spotted Horse reached out for the limbs on the other tree. But with frozen hands, he could not hold on and plummeted through the limbs, unable to slow his fall. He hit the forest floor at an awkward angle, breaking his neck with a loud snap. He lingered still awake, lying flat on his back, arms at his sides, unable to move. The rain fell on his face, and he began to weep and moan pitifully.

Great Bear watched Little Turtle scurry away through the trees and snorted angrily. Puffs of vapor exploded from his muzzle like fire from a dragon's nostrils. The bear rushed forward, easily overtaking the stumbling, injured boy. His jaws fastened around the creature's waist, twisting left and right. He could tell by the smell that this was the one who had tormented him. The puny creature screamed in horror, thrashing and punching his face. This made Great Bear more furious. He chewed, while twisting his jaws left and right, and the body flew apart.

But he was not satisfied.

He viciously tore into each piece, blood and guts flying all over the forest. He ripped the chest open and crushed the head in his massive jaws.

But he was not satisfied.

What little was left, he tore into again and again until only small pieces of flesh and bone remained, and then he ate all of the meat he could find. He enjoyed this type of meat. He enjoyed it a lot—better than any other, and even lapped up the blood.

At the sound of sobbing, he turned to see the other creature still lying at the base of the tree, the wide, fearful eyes fixed on him. He lumbered up to the youth and sniffed the toes. His nose traveled up to the crotch, lingered a second, then the face. The great tongue flicked out, licking off the salty tears. Black Spotted Horse moaned, eyes tight shut. Great Bear gently took the whimpering boy's head and shoulders into his mouth and stood upright. With a flip of his head, the body slid down his throat.

CHAPTER FIVE

Five days later White Crow and seven braves entered the mountains. It was one thing for Little Turtle to go on a secret quest, but quite another for the chief's only son. The trail had been easy to follow, because Black Spotted Horse rode his pony and was not trying to hide, but they lost it in a passing thunderstorm.

The warriors eventually found Little Turtle's first abandoned camp on the southwest side near the river, where he hung out the deer meat to dry. What was he doing here? White Crow wondered.

"Is he on a quest?" one of them asked.

"Maybe he seeks wisdom or guidance from the Great Spirit," another offered.

"I do not know," White Crow admitted, a note of frustration in his voice. "There are prints in the wet sand there, perhaps a week old. Looks like he went south from here. Let us follow this trail and learn more."

On one level, White Crow was worried. He did not know why Little Turtle had not returned to the tribe. Although he had watched him best the wolves out on the prairie, Little Turtle must have had more to do, some task to perform, or something to learn. On another level, it was not unusual for a young man to try and find his place in the world as a warrior. The People did not discourage them. In fact, when he was Little Turtle's age, his father had encouraged his own desire to join the raid against the Arapaho.

They followed a vague trail around to the east side of the mountain range. The next day their horses became restless. White Crow reached up, scratching his horse behind the left ear and cooed softly to calm him. Higher they climbed. They were not in a hurry. And apparently neither was Little Turtle, who seemed to have taken every side trail, however faint. But he always returned to the main trail, as if looking for something. What?

After noon on the third day, they found Black Spotted Horse's pony grazing in a meadow, a rope and stake dragging behind.

"He left his horse near here," White Crow noted. He walked around the meadow but could not find anything definitive.

They staked the horse again—to be picked up later, and slowly rode into a dense part of the forest. The darkness grew until it felt like the sun had set an hour before. A roar shook them to the core. They were all veterans of many battles against other tribes, hunters, trappers, and cavalry patrols. They had all encountered grizzlies and survived to tell stories around the evening fires. But the roar that shook the forest seemed to penetrate their souls.

Suddenly, from up the hill, Great Bear charged into their midst. The great claws swept through their ranks, dismembering three horses and riders. One horse reared in fear, dumping its rider. The bear stepped on the struggling man, crushing the life out of him, while viciously tearing out the throat of the frightened horse. Two warriors threw spears, striking true, which only enraged the bear, and he tore into the desperate men.

White Crow shot two arrows which did not seem to have any effect; the bear ignored them. He desperately kicked his horse's sides and swung away. But the bear also turned to see the fleeing horse, and charged. He easily overtook the pair, and in his monumental rage, tore them apart.

But he was not satisfied.

He walked back down the trail and tore the dead horses and men into little pieces. Then he stood and roared, again and again and again. Frustration, pain, and overwhelming madness foamed in his bloody mouth and mind.

And still he was not satisfied.

For the next two hours, Great Bear walked among the pieces of flesh and bones and ate all of the human warriors. Then he walked up the mountain to the cold, dark cave and slept fitfully.

At the sound of the first roar, the main Cheyenne hunting party out on the prairie, scouting a herd of elk, turned to face the mountain range. They started a slow walk in that direction, but stopped when the roar started again and did not stop. They looked at each other in wonder and fear. Just before dark they came upon the scene of the massacre: the forest all around covered in red blood. A flock of crows, feasting on little pieces of flesh, flew up in protest as the hunting party came upon the scene.

Willow Talks dismounted, walking among the carnage. "That is White Crow's horse," he said without emotion. He could not believe what he was seeing. It felt like a bad dream.

Porcupine Robe said, "This is my brother Red Wolf's horse. But where is Red Wolf? Wait. Ayee! There is his necklace. There is his head band." He moaned and fell to his knees, fingering the blood-soaked objects.

Two Moons Rising dismounted and studied the ground with his fingers. "Look. This print in the bloody mud. A bear did this. But the size…" He gasped and stumbled back involuntarily, eyes bulging and unbelieving, jaw hanging slack.

"Great Bear," Willow Talks murmured. His voice broke. "I…I think…I think Great Bear ate…" He broke off, bent over and vomited. He straightened, wiping his mouth with the back of his hand, but he was not embarrassed.

Two Moons Rising put his hand on his shoulder. "Great Bear—ate them," he choked out.

Black Kettle looked all around, trying to imagine the scene. "Only a demon could do this," he whispered hoarsely. "Would slay and eat its victims."

Porcupine Robe picked up a broken lance then threw it down as if it were white hot. His voice quavered, "Great Bear is on the warpath." A raven squawked and he flinched, his eyes scanning the forest fearfully. "We cannot fight such as this." He waved his arm around the forest. "We cannot win." He mounted his horse.

"The People are doomed," Black Kettle lamented.

"Great Spirit is against us," Willow Talks cried. "We will become no more."

Darkness overtook them as they rode down the mountain at a quick trot. They took nothing of the fallen warriors. They worried that their friends would not find a resting place in the next life after such a gruesome, horrifying death. Some of them moaned softly as they rode away. The Spirit of Great Bear had declared war on them, and they feared for the People. Who could survive? After the horrifying scene, they all feared what the future would bring. If Great Bear was against them, the People would perish from the earth or be much diminished.

The next day a large Ute hunting party spotted the seven warriors crossing the prairie in the distance. They worked their way along a ravine until they were in a good position to ambush the unwary foe. As the Cheyenne approached, the Ute shouted and ran their horses up out of the hidden depression. With loud yells and screams, they attacked.

But the Cheyenne did not respond. They sat on their horses, leaning forward, heads bowed, spears pointed at the ground, their faces and chests covered in dry mud. Some had their eyes closed. Some wept softly.

Angry Buffalo called sharply and held up his hand to stop the attack. They sat their horses, quietly watching as the procession slowly filed past. He looked around at the others. He did not want to speak in the presence of so holy a sight. To those around him, he signed, *something terrible happened.*

Great Bear aimlessly wandered the mountain range. At times he could not sleep and stumbled along disoriented, thoughts hazy and unfocused. When he did sleep, it was as if dead and often lasted two or three days. He didn't eat grasses or leaves or tubers anymore. In his pain and anger, he slaughtered whatever animal was unfortunate enough to cross his path. Soon grizzlies fled at the mere scent or sound of him. The moose, elk, lions, mountain sheep, mountain goats, wolves and others learned to give him a wide berth or left the territory completely.

One evening he awoke in the dark. He had not been in a deep sleep. He stumbled to the cave entrance and sniffed the air. The rain fell hard. But he sensed a new scent floating up the mountain on the swirling wind currents. Although still dark, he easily navigated through the trees and came upon a yearling calf. The creature cried out piteously and tried to run, and this caused a spark of energy to flow through his body. He roared and leapt upon the unfortunate creature. He liked the taste, so he settled in and ate most of it. When satisfied, he worked his way along the hillside and spotted more of the creatures. The beasts called out in fear, and he rushed among them, slashing with his great claws, biting and tearing. He raised up on his hind feet in the heavy rain, sniffing the air.

Suddenly, he reached above his head and tore at the tree next to him, drawing long scratches down the side. This my territory, the deep white marks announced. My land. My home. I define the boundaries. Enter at your own risk. Enter and die.

He stood there for several minutes, unsteady, the rain beating down relentlessly. Lightning struck somewhere up the mountain, quickly followed by a cascading roll of thunder. Different scents wafted by his nose but nothing defined in the downpour. The cattle smell lost its potency then disappeared. The peculiar tang of fresh blood lingered at his feet but even that began to fade, washed away. In the back of his mind, he understood that there were more of the creatures nearby, down the hill, but he felt woozy with sleep, and the fatigue of his gnawing wound. He crawled back up the hill into the back of his cave, and slept hard.

CHAPTER SIX

Three days later the bear lay on the west ridge crest, looking down on the distant river. His vision blurred temporarily then cleared. A small herd of two hundred buffalo charged across the river, harried by a pack of large timber wolves. They caught a calf midstream. Great Bear could just hear the calf bawling in fear, as they dragged her down. In the afternoon, the bear stood unsteadily and walked back down the east side toward his cave. From somewhere down below, he heard a horse neigh. His ears twitched and he stood, sniffing the air all around. He had not smelled horse in a long time. It reminded him of something. He tensed; red eyes narrowed. His nose twitched. The smell of humans swirled about with that of horse, and he grunted in growing rage. He walked purposefully down the hill, not in a hurry, head lowered, eyes glazed over in vengeful, black madness.

José Bonegas and Raul Pascual laughed lightly. Just another bear, the vaqueros thought. They had worked on the Don Pedro Garcia rancho in central Texas all their life and had roped many grizzlies and wolves—just about anything that could be roped had been roped, even a sidewinder rattlesnake one time. All they needed was a challenge, or a dare, and off they charged.

In this case, Raul's brother, Pablo, along with James McKay, Philip Two Feathers, William O'Keefe, and Thomas Rhodes were out one morning, looking for cattle scattered from the herd by the thunderstorm during the night. They found some killed by a grizzly—a calf eaten, the others slaughtered—and sprinted back to the cattle drive with their tails tucked between their legs, or so the vaqueros interpreted the story. The fearful men said the grizzly was too big to be roped. A monster out of nightmares. Too big for anything.

They hadn't actually seen the bear, but Pablo tried to explain to his brother how big the bear's paw was. When he drew the outline in the dirt—twenty inches long, they laughed harder. It was unbelievably huge. Magnificently huge. El grande! But for Raul and José, always ropable. To them, any animal could be roped. Then they would drag his sorry carcass back to the others, and parade him around like the trophy he was.

Okay, maybe he was big. Maybe he was very big. But with ropes binding his body tightly, they would drag him along until he decided to cooperate. Simple. Such was their experience so many times before. They knew what to do, and their wonderful horses even understood. Between the four of them, they would humbly accept the accolades of their amazing—as always—success. Well, maybe not so humbly. They both loved to brag about their exploits in and out of the saddle.

"Do you remember that big wolf outside Santa Fe?" José asked.

Raul huffed a giggle. "Sí, El Diablo Lobo. Devil Wolf. Old scar face. Now that one was biiiig." He extended the word *big* into a long sing-song word.

José smiled. "Exactly. Killed sheep just for fun. Ah, and that poor sheep farmer." He crossed himself twice, and picked up his crucifix and kissed it.

"We made some money on that deal," Raul said, remembering the epic battle.

"Sí, and I have the scars still." José pulled back his left sleeve to reveal the pink bite marks, even after two years.

"You would have been okay, if you hadn't fallen off your horse," Raul taunted. "Then he pounced on you like a little lamb."

José grinned at the memory. "Sí, I was...clumsy that day." His old horse backed over a log and tripped, and they fell in a heap. He would never think to blame his wonder horse.

Raul did not expect José's admission of weakness or failure; it wasn't really his fault after all. Still, they caught the big wolf and dragged it back to town—ten miles. Amazingly, it was still alive, snarling, and just as mean. A demon beast. The townspeople said it was the biggest wolf anyone had ever seen. They put it in a pit with two dozen mean javelinas, and the betting was just as fierce.

"Do you have any of the reward money left?" José asked.

"Sí, all of it—one hundred dollars—gold. The Don keeps it in the safe for me. And you?"

"You know I bought that new saddle and bridle." He would not admit to Raul that he had lost the rest gambling. It had been two years after all. But the fact that Raul saved his money impressed him greatly, although he would not say anything. Maybe he should put some money aside. All his life he spent what he earned and didn't have more than two or three American silver dollars on him at any given moment.

They crossed the river and set up camp where the cattle drive had stopped during the thunderstorm. The forest was eerily quiet. No birds called or squirrels chittered like in other places. The horses seemed agitated and restless, ears twitching, soft snorts, eyes alert. They kept the fire small, just enough to heat the water for coffee. Neither slept deeply and were up an hour before sunrise.

"I just want to catch that bear and get out of this place," José said softly, scanning the forest around them. "Too quiet for me."

Raul threw the saddle over his horse's back. "Sí, feels like before a storm—quiet, heavy."

They walked their horses along a thin game trail. José chewed on a piece of jerky and wished for the hundredth time that he had a rifle or pistola. The vaqueros almost never carried firearms. He was not doubting their ability to rope the bear, but if something went wrong—you never know. He shook his head, trying to eject his doubts.

Raul looked back at him, smiling. "Nervous?"

José frowned. "What? Me?"

Raul nodded knowingly. "Yeah, me too."

"Look there!" José called, but not loudly. "A dead bull." He rode up to the bull and looked around. "Cows over there."

"Sí, and the calf over there, well, what's left of him."

"So much blood…" José began.

A loud but distant roar up the mountain caused them to turn suddenly. Their horses skittered sideways, heads tossing, snorting in fear. The vaqueros began twirling their lassos loosely, at the ready. Raul tried to smile, but it came out as a grimace, eyes fearful, his stomach in his throat. His lasso clipped a tree branch.

"Down the hill—there!" Raul shouted. "Let's go. That open space before the rocks. More room."

The sound of something crashing into trees and tearing through the brush grew louder. It sounded like a large boulder had broken off and was careening down the side of the mountain. They turned their horses and sprinted down the hill. Although the area was open, they were still on the side of the steep mountain. They turned to confront the bear, as it broke into the open at a dead run.

José felt his blood turn cold. Holy Mother of God, he thought. Pablo was right. The bear was absolutely huge—a monster, indeed. He automatically threw the lasso while spurring his horse, so it leapt like a rabbit, out of the charging bear's path. The lasso fell expertly over the bear's wide head.

On the other side, Raul threw his lasso around the bear's head and his horse squatted back on its heels, while Raul looped the rope around the saddle horn. Now they had the bear immobilized between them. For a few precious seconds.

"Ee ha!" Raul shouted in victory, waving his sombrero over his head. "Nothing to it."

But José gulped in fear and could not speak or respond. He realized they were in a fight for their lives. His horse tried to spring forward, dirt flying, but could not actually move, the rope taut.

The great bear suddenly stood on its hind legs, which abruptly dragged both horses closer. The horses lunged, repeatedly, trying to move away from the bear, but slid back instead. The bear turned quickly, swiping at the rope with its right paw, not the claws, which jerked Raul's horse backwards and within striking range. The left paw swept around, tearing the horse's head off. The bear fell upon Raul, viciously tearing into his abdomen. Raul held the bear's muzzle in his hands, screaming in horror as the bear chewed.

José wished he had a rifle. Ten rifles. An army. He swung his horse around, pulling the bear off Raul's mutilated body. He spurred the horse viciously. The bear followed at first, but not because it was being pulled along. José yelled and whooped, slapping his white stallion's flank with his sombrero.

"I drag you!" he cried. "I drag you down the hill! I drag you back to hell!" He reined his horse to the left, hoping to bind the rope tightly around the bear, immobilizing the arms.

The bear grunted in surprise, as the rope pulled him around. The horse was strong, digging in and lunging, dirt spraying up behind, desperate, nostrils flared in abject fear and determination. Again, the bear did not cut the rope with his claws, but swiped at it with his right paw, suddenly yanking the frightened horse over and onto its back. José tumbled to the ground but deftly rolled up onto the balls of his feet.

The bear slashed the horse with its claws and stood, towering over José. The vaquero screamed and raised his arms protectively over his head. The bear leaned over, roaring just feet away, covering José in bloody slobber. José peed. The great jaws snapped at José, but the vaquero dived between the massive legs and ran down the hill. At first Great Bear was confused, looking left and right, then he heard the vaquero behind him and turned.

José sprinted down the hill, screaming over and over, "O Dios mío. Mary, Joseph and Jesus, save me!" Without looking back, he scrambled up the rocks and leapt into the air—the ground thirty feet below. In his hysteria, he didn't care about falling or landing or being hurt—just getting away. But as his feet left the ground, the great bear's jaws fastened around his waist.

José cried and thrashed. The bear slowly carried him back up the hill until it stood over the whimpering, struggling stallion. He chewed the vaquero in half, the two pieces falling on the horse. His pink small intestines draped over the bear's lower jaw, down both sides. Using his arms, José crawled up to the horse's head and kissed the face repeatedly, sobbing. José held onto his horse's right ear with both hands as the bear rolled him over, tilted his torso up and slurped out his liver and heart. The horse continued to whimper and struggle, so the bear bit down savagely, ripping out its throat, the body quivering and kicking in its death throes.

Raul could not move, but his arms flailed in the air. "If I had a rifle, I shoot you!" he cried hysterically.

The bear spun back around. He walked up to Raul and buried his face in the abdomen, slurping up the guts. Raul screamed, "No! Stop! I beg you!" He beat at the face desperately and pulled at the fur. The bear casually

81

rolled him over and began eating the buttocks and legs, tearing off great strips of meat. "No more, please no more!" Raul cried pitifully. Finally, with the loss of blood, he began to fade. "Please—no more...please." As Great Bear bit into his back, Raul's last breath faded away.

When most of Raul was gone, Great Bear stood on his hind legs and roared again and again, turning in a circle, bloody foam dripping off his red muzzle. He roared out his ancestral majesty, his primal superiority, and the certain victory at his bloody feet.

Slowly the madness ebbed. The sounds of birds flitting through the nearby bushes and tree limbs returned. A jay called. Two ravens dropped down by the head of Raul's horse, closely inspecting the staring right eye. The wind picked up, caressing the forest with sighs and groans as the trees swayed, sounding eerily like a mournful dirge. Finally, Great Bear dropped to all fours and wandered up the hill to his cave, where he slept heavily.

Late the next day, Great Bear heard a distant noise. Crows. A murder of crows called incessantly, and it irritated him. He rose slowly, shaking his great hide and walked to the cave entrance.

Far down the hill, he thought he heard a new sound. A creature was crying out in anguish. For some reason this annoyed him to his core. He felt compelled to make it stop. Wait! What was that scent wafting up the side of the mountain? He stood on his hind feet, nose twitching, closely inspecting the air currents. His eyes grew large and he grunted as the desire for human flesh overwhelmed his senses. He could not get enough. A great flow of drool fell from his massive jaws, still bloody pink from the day before. With a loud huff, he launched himself off the ledge and down the side of the mountain.

His rage grew and his speed increased, until he stopped trying to dodge trees and brush, but instead crashed through everything. Like a boulder careening down the side of the mountain, he created a new path of destruction, snapping off trees, straight toward his unwary prey.

There they are! Fleeing! Some running left, but two straight ahead. A horse, and a human on another horse. He picked up speed, his eyes flashing with the lust for human flesh. The black stallion in the lead jumped over the mass of logs, and the other horse with the creature on its back followed, flying through the air to safety beyond, but they dropped something. Great Bear slid to a stop. At his feet lay a shiny object. In his rage, he roared and tore the shiny silver saddle into little pieces.

CHAPTER SEVEN

ll in all, the cattle drive was successful. They departed the Don Pedro Garcia rancho on March 11th, 1866 and arrived in Denver on April 30th—over six long weeks. Robert Garcia Preston and James William McKay were the official owners and leaders of the drive, but James' half would be divided evenly between his partners: Henry, Gideon, Josiah and Michael.

Henry was James' younger brother by two years, and James had just turned twenty in April. Henry turned eighteen in May, but looked and acted much older—the benefit of a few of life's harder lessons in recent years. Gideon turned twenty in May, and Josiah would be twenty in December. Both were born as free black men, raised on the McKay plantation outside Asheville, North Carolina. Michael Tall Corn was a Shawnee, who joined the McKay Rangers shortly after they formed the unit in the last year of the Civil War—almost two years before. Michael was the oldest at twenty-two. Gideon was the blacksmith's son and had the thick arms to prove it. He was much darker than Josiah, who became an ordained minister just before they left North Carolina. They all married sweethearts at the end of the war, except Michael.

They formed the McKay Rangers after a Union patrol massacred the McKay family on suspicion of aiding and hiding bushwhackers. Over time the McKay Rangers killed the leaders of that wretched patrol, then settled down to keep the Asheville area safe from Union army patrols and foragers, renegades, guerillas, and deserters. They were so deadly that Union troops learned to avoid the area. The Union army attempted to kill the rangers many times, but they always eluded the enemy or killed them outright. So it was easy, after the war, for the Union to keep the bounties on bushwhackers in effect.

Although the war was over, the McKay Rangers fled for their lives. Almost two weeks after they crossed the Green River on the southern border of North Carolina, a Union cavalry patrol learned what they had done and gave chase. To avoid capture, the rangers split up: three wagons heading southeast at first, the other two moving due south, then west. The chase was often close and personal, the patrols breathing hard down their necks at every turn. Robert joined James and Gideon in Georgia and helped them get to Texas.

When the wagons finally arrived at their destination of New Braunfels, Texas—northeast of San Antonio—the cavalry patrol caught up with them. But the vengeful captain could not get any of his men to arrest the fugitives. The troopers had grown to respect the rangers and their desire to put the Civil War behind them. The captain's fiancée was in town and coaxed him into giving up the chase—for the time being. The McKay Rangers settled down to civilian life.

Robert's grandfather, Don Pedro Garcia, in appreciation for all the McKay Rangers had done to help his grandson, gave them a northern portion of his great ranch—50,000 acres *each*. Workers from the rancho helped build adobe homes for everyone, and Michael started a general store in town.

With over a million longhorns running wild, it was only natural that the young men go to work gathering cattle for a drive to market. Robert found a buyer in Colorado, who would pay top dollar, if they could get the herd there in early spring. They spent all winter gathering wild cattle and set off in mid-March, arriving in Denver at the end of April.

During the drive, about half way to their destination, they holed up in the Sangre de Cristo mountain range during a fierce storm. During the night, they heard a bear roar up the mountain. The bear killed some cattle and ate a calf. Two of the vaqueros rode back to rope what they thought would be a regular grizzly, a trick they had performed many times in the past. When James learned they went back to rope the bear, he, Philip, and Washington T. Jefferson gave chase. Raul's brother, Pablo, followed. They found where the big bear had killed the vaqueros, a very disturbing sight, because so little remained. Pablo arrived shortly after and cried out when he saw the massacre. But he retrieved his brother's famous silver saddle.

As they started to ride away, the roar of the bear and his rapid approach caused them to flee for their lives. Barely. Pablo lost the saddle, jumping his horse over a log jam. He turned to see the bear tearing up the saddle, as if made of thin tissue paper. After that, he quit the cattle drive and rode home.

Michael, Henry and Gideon joined the herd two weeks before it arrived in Denver and missed the incident with the bear.

Although the cattle drive had to battle the weather, bandits, and Indians, they arrived with most of the cattle, and others carefully gathered out of a buffalo herd. As the first cattle herd into Denver that spring, they also received top dollar for their effort, although at the end of a gun battle in the Planter House saloon.

For the wounded, convalescence lasted until the end of the third week in May. James had been shot in the side but was mostly back to normal, although a little stiff in the morning. Robert still could not sit up straight, favoring his left butt cheek, where the unerring bullet found its home. He rode his horse by mostly standing or leaning in the saddle. Henry and Michael were shot in the chest, but Henry bounced back quickly, out of action for only one week. Michael, though, suffered from a shot to the upper left lung; his recovery painfully slow.

They made only ten miles a day, pushing their little herd of fifty-one special cattle. The bretagne bull proudly led the group of longhorn cows and his bretagne-longhorn-cross calves.

While driving the herd north, they had found the bretagne cattle on a homestead that had been attacked by Comanches, the family tortured and killed. In the family bible, recovered from the ruins of the burned-out sod house, they found a receipt for the bull and sent money back east to the relatives, as if they had sold the bull and cattle to themselves. They determined that the bretagne bull would produce higher quality calves for the market the following year.

Grim-faced and solemn, Michael sat on the wagon seat next to Ortega, the cook. He had dark brown, shoulder length hair, with an old floppy hat of an indistinct earthen color pulled down low over his brow—his brown eyes deep in shadow. He brooded, arms crossed, gently rocking left and right, while chewing on an unlit cigar.

From James' description of the bear, he could imagine what they were headed for. It would be an epic hunt. The most dangerous any of them had ever faced, not counting their encounter with Mr. Cooper, back when they were rangers during the Civil War. That mountain man had almost ended them. No, he would need all the strength he could muster between now and then. Although he could have ridden his horse, he always felt tired and knew he needed to continue healing, so he sat back and enjoyed the wagon seat. On occasion, he lay in the back in a hammock Robert had fashioned for him. By his reckoning, they would be at the southern tip of the Sangre de Cristo mountains in about fourteen days—end of the first week of June.

He took the cigar out of his mouth and thoughtfully studied the chewed end. A coyote yipped in the draw off to the right and, out of habit, he studied the area carefully. They needed a plan.

James' horse plodded along in no particular hurry. The late morning sun felt good. The rain the day before kept the dust down. James sat the saddle easily. He was all of six feet tall and lean from hard work and life on the trail. His long brown hair, with streaks of blond, hung down beyond his shirt collar. Even as a boy, he had preferred to wear it long, so his mother was always after him to cut it.

"Michael doesn't have to cut his hair," he had whined.

"Michael is an Indian, Jimmy, so he doesn't have to cut it," his mother scolded.

He wore two Colt revolvers, a habit the Rangers developed out of necessity, when they needed a lot of firepower at short notice. He wore a new wide-brimmed brown felt hat, dusty now, purchased in Denver after the cattle drive. He had found a golden eagle feather and thread it through the banding. He shaved every day, regardless—a nod to his father. Pa thought the boys should start shaving as soon as the peach fuzz appeared, but was less concerned about the length of the hair on their heads. He often said, in one form or another, "Many of our founding fathers wore their hair long, but they shaved their faces to instill the importance of a civilized appearance and education." When Ma scolded him about the length of his hair, he looked to his pa for support, but the old fellow merely winked and looked away, not wanting any part of *that* battle.

As the Sangre de Cristo mountains came into view, James felt a sense of foreboding that lingered like an achy tooth. "Maybe we should let the bear go," he suggested to Henry, riding on his right.

"Your call." Henry was used to James throwing out a thought or idea to see what he thought about it. Although two years younger, like James he was tall, a little lanky, wide shouldered, and sat the saddle as if he'd been born to it. He kept his hair short, getting it cut in town once every three months or less. When it overlapped his collar and ears, it was time to go in, although Ortega cut it once on the drive. Like James, he shaved daily, rain or shine, cold water or hot. He would lather up with a bar of soap and scrape the new growth off with the straight razor. Out of habit, he could dry shave while riding his horse, which was easier if done daily, and the beard did not have a chance to thicken and toughen up. And like James he wore two Colt revolvers for quick, decisive action and added firepower. With the war only a year behind them, the habits that had kept them alive were not to be cast aside lightly. The world was still a dangerous place, and a sixth or seventh bullet, in quick succession, might be the difference between life and death. It wasn't a fancy rig, just simple and useful, and occasionally necessary.

"You're not very helpful," James said sullenly.

"It's *your* call. I could go either way. I came *after* the bear killed those boys, so I don't have a horse in this race—not really." He meant not personally, although he felt an overall obligation as an owner of the drive.

James huffed a knowing chuckle. "You might before this is over."

"Sounds like you're on the fence about our little hunt."

"I am. Don't know what made the bear so mean, but I'm not sure we can kill it before it kills all or most of us."

The idea that the bear could kill everyone gave Henry pause. This was no ordinary bear, if what James had said around the campfire was true. It was bigger and meaner than any creature they had ever encountered. "So, you want to dodge the bear and avoid what you think will be certain death." He wore a lopsided grin. He thought the idea a little funny; it was only a bear after all.

James looked at him and sighed. "Yeah. Something like that." He wanted to smile, but a frown developed instead. Henry had hit it right.

Henry studied his horse's ears. "You know you didn't force anyone to come along."

"I know. But no one would argue if I said we should forget the bear and head on home."

"True enough. If it's weighing on you, why don't we just bypass these mountains? You're the trail boss."

James searched his heart, trying to come up with a plausible answer. He felt trapped. "Well, we promised Pablo we would kill the bear that killed his brother, Raul, and our friend José. I promised him. Me."

Henry nodded slowly. "There it is. You feel trapped by a promise. Obligated," he said, finally beginning to understand. "Josiah said the bible says that the man who keeps his oath even when it hurts can dwell in God's sanctuary."

"Where does it say that?"

"Psalm fifteen, verse four."

James looked back at the herd before speaking. "But I've never backed away from a promise, or telling the truth, even when it hurt. I guess it's like those soldiers who march into battle, knowing they are likely to die."

Now Henry rode along in silence, digesting that ominous idea. "Wait a minute. You don't know that. It's a bear, for goodness' sake. A mean bear, granted. A big bear by all accounts, but it is still a God-created bear.

Why just a little over a year ago, we set up ambushes for Union infantry and cavalry, and came away unscathed. We invited the devil himself to join us for a few months and came through—well, mostly unharmed." He remembered how Mr. Cooper betrayed them, and the Union soldiers had beaten him to within an inch of death. "What I'm saying is, let's approach this bear killing business as a military mission; a McKay Ranger ambush mission, and not a simple hunting trip for a killer bear. Because from all you said, if we think this is a simple hunting trip, then we will probably be in trouble before we start."

James nodded. He had been thinking about the problem all wrong—as a big hunt. Henry was right. This would have to be a military mission with clear objectives, detailed tactics, necessary contingency plans, an exit plan, and a definition of success—*a dead bear*. "You're right." His mind began to race as it shifted from a hunting trip to a military style mission. We can do this, he thought.

Blackie's head came up sharply and his ears twitched forward. Three Indians appeared on horseback, trotting out of the draw to their front right—the west side, three hundred yards. James shook his head in amazement. There could be a hundred Cheyenne in there, and they would not know until too late. They had two scouts further out front, Gideon and O'Keefe, but they had missed this group.

"Look friendly enough," Henry noted dryly, absently pulling the loop off his right pistol hammer. He noticed James did the same.

"I think they're Cheyenne," James said.

"How can you tell?"

"The way they ride. Headbands. Markings on their horses.

The three Indians pulled up to wait.

Without taking his eyes off the Indians, James said, "Why don't you go find Philip Two Feathers." Philip was the best scout. He would have Philip scout ahead in the future, although he might not have discovered this group either.

Henry wheeled his horse around and raced off.

James looked behind for Robert but couldn't see him. Must be in back somewhere.

As he drew near, the Indian in the middle raised his hand. James raised his and moved to within fifty feet. The Indian in the middle was big, wide shouldered, with deep set, dark eyes. As the Indian's horse shifted, James noticed that the buckskin had a cavalry brand. The

Cheyenne looked on patiently, neither friendly nor aggressive.

James could hear Henry coming with Philip. They arrived in a cloud of dust. James turned. Beyond them, he could see other riders racing toward them from the herd. They moved to within ten feet.

Philip quickly signed with the lead Indian then turned to James. "Want cows."

James shook his head. "Tell them this is a special herd we are taking home to Texas. When we come through next time, I will give them many cows."

Philip signed all of this.

The Indian shook his head angrily. He started to turn his horse away, when James said, "Wait."

He turned back.

"Philip, tell him we go to kill Warpath Bear."

When the herd came through a few months before, they gave some cows to the Cheyenne, and the chief told them to avoid Warpath Bear in the mountains to their west. That was after the bear had already killed some of their cattle during the thunderstorm and tornado.

Philip signed, and the Indian frowned and shook his head. His signs were angry and quick, but James thought he also saw a hint of fear.

Philip translated, "Warpath Bear cannot be killed. Wise men go around his mountains. Fools enter."

"Ask him if he has heard about *Diablos con Rifles Largos*." [Devils with Long Rifles] When the rangers were fleeing the cavalry patrol, they had held off the Comanche by shooting at them from long distances. The Comanche quickly learned to leave them alone, and gave them that name.

The Indian looked closely at James then back at the herd. He signed and Philip said, "He ask, you are *Diablos con Rifles Largos?*"

James nodded slightly.

No one said anything for a full minute. James could hear the riders from the herd slow, walking their horses toward the group.

James pointed to his chest then the mountains. "I kill Warpath Bear."

Philip started to sign, but the Indian raised his right hand for him to stop. He looked intently at James, then nodded with approval. "Okay," he said and rode off.

"Did he understand us the whole time?" Henry asked.

Philip looked confused and shrugged. "Might have."

Robert and the other four rode up.

"I know what he's thinking," James said. "If we kill the bear, they get to hunt that territory again. If the bear kills us, they get the herd. Either way, they win."

Henry watched the Indians fall into a trot, moving due east. "You might be right."

Robert rode up alongside James. "Trouble?"

"Not really. Wanted cows. Told him we were going to kill the warpath bear, and he looked skeptical."

"For good reason. Heard that last part, where he wins either way it turns out."

"The Cheyenne will probably leave us alone, but let's double the guard anyhow."

CHAPTER EIGHT

Two days later they arrived at the southern end of the Sangre de Cristo mountains.

"I don't wanna get too close," Robert said. "The cattle might tempt the ole varmint. I mean, afore we're ready and all."

"Want to set up camp out here on the prairie?" James asked. He didn't have a preference or a firm plan yet.

Robert looked around. "Wish we had more wagons; somethin' we could circle to make a more defensible position." Robert spent three years with Terry's Rangers during the Civil War and rose to the rank of First Sergeant.

James said, "We've got enough people to protect the herd, unless another tornado comes through or stampeding buffalo."

"I was thinkin' partly of Indians but mostly about that devil bear."

"Well, if you saw that pawprint and scratch marks, you'd know a hundred wagons in a circle wouldn't stop the critter. Would only make him mad and more determined than ever."

With his eyes, Robert measured the distance to the mountains. "Three miles out from the beginnin' of the foothills should be 'nough."

"Then about right here?" James asked, judging the distance also.

"Yeah, reckon so." He didn't sound convinced.

That evening around the fire, they talked about their options.

O'Keefe said, "Since we know the beastie is easily angered by intruders, we should run a few cows up there into them hills, you know, to sorta use'm as bait."

"Ah, I see," said Henry. "Bait for our ambush."

"Exactly my thinkin'."

"What do you say, Robert?" Henry asked.

Robert looked at James and shrugged. "Can use the regular longhorn cows, none as carryin' calves at this point. We can get plenty more of those."

James added, "And the ones close to weening their calves. I can think of three or four like that."

"So, we use a few cows," Gideon said. "But we need to stake them to a spot of our choosing, with overlapping fields of fire: an open area down the hill from the forest."

"That's the idea," Josiah said, "Like when we ambushed Captain Caldwell and his patrol at Anderson Bridge."

Henry said, "Exactly. We can dig hide positions. That way, if the bear doesn't die sudden like, it won't really know who shot it or have a specific person to attack."

"What?" Gideon asked skeptically. "You think that if the four of us shoot our long rifles at him, he will survive? If we each get two or three shots off, he won't have a chance. Why if he attacked any one of us, the others would fill him so full of lead, he wouldn't be able to walk. I don't care how big he thinks he is."

James chuckled lightly, shaking his head. "Hold on there, Mr. Gideon. Let me show you something." He knelt down by the fire. With a stick he cut a trench in the dirt. When finished, he poked five holes in front, then took off his boot and set it down in the middle of the crude drawing. The print was twenty-two inches long, and the five holes for the claw tips were eight inches beyond. "That, my friend, is the bear's paw print. I can attest the size is fairly accurate."

"Not possible," Josiah whispered. "It's huge, like one of them dino-saurs that fellow William Parker Foulke discovered a few years back in New Jersey—a hadro-saurus, I think."

"Aye, lad, the stuff of nightmares," O'Keefe added. He remembered seeing that paw print up in the woods, and it still scared him. He knew what a grizzly could do, and he knew there was no creature on earth more dangerous, or more deadly.

"I see what you mean," Gideon said flatly. "It's not like anything we've ever dealt with before."

"Unpredictable's the word your really lookin' for," Robert said.

"Not really unpredictable," Michael added, entering the conversation for the first time.

"What do you mean?" Robert asked.

"When the McKay Rangers ambushed Union patrols, we studied them, got to know their habits, routes, preferences. When the time came, they were predictable to us, even if they deviated from their normal routine a little. We knew them well enough that any changes were anticipated and planned for."

James started nodding. "We should study the bear first."

Michael looked over at him. "We should study the bear."

"Get to know our enemy," Robert said. "An old military maxim, I learned durin' the war."

"It would *not* be like studying a Union patrol," Henry argued. "Those boys could not sniff the wind, catch your scent, and chase you down for supper."

"Michael and Henry are right," James said. "We need to know our enemy, but it is possible that in the study the observers or scouts might get killed."

"Okay, we gotta be special careful like," Robert conceded.

"So, Michael," Henry began, "Do you want to ease on up there into those hills with me and scout around?" To Henry, it was still just a bear. He could not imagine a bear the size of the print. When they were young, he and James had outrun a grizzly they surprised in the woods. They zigged and zagged through the trees, and the old boar just gave up. In his mind, he imaged a similar scenario. They would find the bear, figure where he ranged, and set up an ambush. Kill the brute. Nice and neat. Then head home.

"With binoculars." Unlike Henry, Michael was worried. He had talked to Philip Two Feathers, Thomas Rhodes, and O'Keefe, who had all been with James the day they found the slaughtered cattle and the monster paw print. Every one of them spoke of the print and territorial scratch marks with a sort of reverence and awe. Especially O'Keefe, who had seen a grizzly kill an African lion and Bengal tiger in a California gold mining town.

O'Keefe told him, "This here bear is twice the size of that gold camp grizzly. He is not just bigger, he's maybe twice the size. I mean it, laddie, he's uncanny large and dangerous."

James looked off toward the mountains. "In the morning let's head over there and set up a day camp down the hill in a good defensible location. If the scouting goes awry, the scouts can run toward the camp and get help from the long guns."

"Like when Gideon and Michael ran back to our cave after spying on the Union camp two Christmas' ago," Josiah said. A band of cavalry soldiers chased Gideon and Michael across a snowy field, but they knew the others would be up on the ridge watching for them. As predicted, James, Henry and Josiah shot the troopers to pieces.

"Exactly. We'll set up fields of fire, put out range markers so we know the distances, and flags so we can calculate the wind, and stay ready."

Philip stood. "Two scout teams. Michael and Henry, me and Josiah."

"Makes sense," Michael said. "We can go up the mountain at different places but be ready to run back to the camp."

"We'll have different people scout, so everyone gets a chance that wants it," James said.

"I wish we had horns," Henry said. "You know, to like, alert the camp we are running in, and all."

"Hear you before we see you," Gideon said. "An alert that you're in trouble."

"That's right."

"I think O'Keefe's got a trumpet," Robert volunteered.

O'Keefe had not been paying attention. He had no plans to hunt the bear and could not shoot well enough to mount a defense at the day camp. He would keep watch over the little herd and stay out of it. "What?" he asked, looking up from the fire.

Henry said cheerfully, "We want to use your trumpet, if we have to run back to the camp with the bear on our tails." In actuality, he thought that if he was running for his life with a monster bear breathing down his neck, he probably wouldn't have the breath to blow a bugle, riding a horse or not.

"Sure," O'Keefe said, waving his left hand nonchalantly. "Take it. Might be useful."

"If we can find a longhorn skull or a buffalo skull," Thomas Rhodes started, "I can make a bugle from a horn."

"We don't need everyone to watch the cattle all the time," Wizzy said. "Some of us can look around the prairie tomorrow for a skull."

"Aye, we can take turns," O'Keefe added. He walked over to his things and came back with the old army trumpet. "Who wants it?"

"Here, let me see that," Michael said, standing. He took the trumpet from O'Keefe, came to attention, and blew a loud and crisp *reveille*.

O'Keefe came to attention and saluted sharply. When Michael finished, O'Keefe shouted, "Top'a the mornin' to ya, General darlin'!"

The men laughed.

"Where'd you learn to do that?" Henry asked Michael, truly impressed.

"I have many hidden talents, *darlin'*," Michael answered mysteriously.

Everyone chuckled.

James stood and walked around the fire. "Tomorrow, let's find likely spots for day camps or rendezvous points along the base of the range, study the options, contingency plans, and sort of plan out the week."

"I like the idea of the rendezvous points," Gideon began. "Start in the south and work our way up the east side of the mountain range, because we know the bear probably has a den or something on this side, I'm guessing."

James looked around at the group. No one disagreed or added anything. "We'll head out right after we eat in the morning."

"Who all is going?" Henry asked.

James studied the group. "Myself and Gideon at a minimum in the day camp on alert to help the scouts. Rifles primed and ready. Tomorrow will be Philip with Josiah, and Michael with you."

Robert chewed on a hard biscuit and raised his cup of coffee. "I'll go."

Thomas B. Rhodes stood. "That big bear sure scares me some, but I'm not afraid to scout the critter."

"That's enough people," James said. "Robert can float between the day camp and herd, in case we need more people there, or people are needed back here. Thomas, you switch off with Henry, and go with Michael every other day."

Wizzy was relatively new, joining them in the last month of the drive. And he was sixteen. "I'd like to help, but I don't know what I could do," he admitted. He wanted to do more than keep O'Keefe company watching the herd all day.

James looked at him. He needed to give the young man a tough job, a man's job. "You will spell any of the scouts, so come along. That leaves, Washington, Emilio, Gustaf and William O'Keefe to watch the herd, with Juan, Whipple and Marcus on hand, and Robert and Wizzy shuttling between, as needed."

"Sounds about right," Robert said. "I'd be happy to lend my Henry rifle to the scouts, if they need it. Philip?"

Philip nodded. "Thanks."

CHAPTER NINE

The sky was light but the sun had not yet cleared the horizon. Long yellow wisps of high clouds stretched from southwest to northeast. Juan Ortega dished up fresh biscuits with bubbling hot bacon gravy. Everyone wanted seconds. The scouts left as the hazy sun cast long shadows across the prairie.

Part of James wanted to ride right to the original place where they lost the cattle during the storm a few months back, find the bear, and kill it outright. Massive firepower. But then that would be just the opposite of what they had planned. They could wander up there looking for the bear and be slaughtered, no matter how many rifles and revolvers they had. The McKay Rangers survived the last year of the war, because they were very careful and thorough. They scouted their enemy and made plans. And that was how he would kill the bear and get these people safely home. He hoped.

They rode south for an hour to the end of the Sangre de Cristo mountain range and studied the terrain. They found a likely place that would work as a temporary base camp with good fields of fire up into the tree line, but with enough open space to engage an attacking bear from multiple angles. Using the horses, they dragged down several small fallen trees and big limbs to use as rests for their rifles.

Michael and Henry moved into the woods on the west side of the range, and Philip and Josiah moved up the east side ridge. The two groups were gone all day. Late in the afternoon, Michael and Henry came back first, then Philip and Josiah.

"Saw some old Indian sign," Michael said.

"Nothing fresh, though," Henry added.

"Some Indian pony tracks," Philip said.

Josiah sat his horse. "The woods are awfully quiet."

"What do you mean?" James asked.

"Noticed it, too," Henry said. "Like the birds and animals just took off or something. Not counting a few mangy ravens and crows."

"That's what I mean," Josiah said. "We didn't see deer tracks or anything else."

"You're both saying you expected to see more and hear more," James said.

"I've lived in the woods all my life," Michael said, "and these woods seem..." He paused looking off toward the hills. "Troubled."

Philip nodded thoughtfully, not speaking. The woods were unusually quiet, but he sensed something lingering in the background, perhaps a deep sadness. A few years back, he had experienced a similar feeling at a Comanche massacre site. They had wiped out a wagon train of Oregon Trail settlers, killing everyone. He thought he might have inherited a sensitivity to certain things from his Shaman father.

During the day, Wizzy found a longhorn skull near the herd. Thomas Rhodes smiled to see it and went to work. As he and Wizzy sat around the fire, he removed the hollow horn from the skull and began carving a mouthpiece at the tip. "Gotta cut back to about here," he explained to Wizzy, "so it comes out roughly the size of the trumpet mouthpiece when done. See that?" He held up the old trumpet and the horn together.

Thomas kept the army trumpet the first day to be sure of the dimensions, and to carve the first horn mouthpiece properly. Wizzy picked it up and blew; a pitiful screech of forced air interrupted the natural quiet of the prairie.

Thomas said, "Purse your lips and make a sound like this." Without using O'Keefe's horn, he put his lips together and blew, sputtering. "Keep doing that and put the horn up there."

Wizzy blew until he was red in the face and an assortment of loud and obnoxious sounds erupted from the trumpet. "You're trying too hard," Thomas said. "Soft like."

Wizzy kept trying and the sound improved — some.

In the evening, Thomas handed the finished bull's horn to Michael. "Here, try this."

Michael held the longhorn, studying the details. Thomas had deftly but perfectly carved a person on horseback roping a steer. "Thomas, this is a fine work of art." He turned the eighteen-inch longhorn all around, studying the details, then put it to his lips and blew a long, deep, plaintive note that carried over the prairie.

"Wow," Wizzy said, truly impressed. "That sounded good."

"Key of A," O'Keefe muttered to himself from behind the chuck wagon.

Michael handed the horn to James. He turned it over, studying the workmanship.

"Thomas," James started. "Would you make more of these horns?"

"Sure," he replied happily. "How many?"

James looked around. "One for this camp. One for the day camp. Then enough for each person in the scout

114

teams. We'll give O'Keefe his horn back, so that would be five more."

"Gonna need a few more skulls," Thomas noted.

James looked at Wizzy. "Think you can handle that order?"

"I'll get on it first thing," Wizzy promised, smiling. He wanted Thomas to make him one, too.

Michael made a mental note to talk to Thomas about making horns for his general store. They had a practical application, and the kids would love them. If Thomas taught other people how to make the horns, he could sell them in other towns.

The next day they moved five miles north on the east side and set up the day camp in a likely location. They decided to concentrate on the east side of the mountain range. Philip and Robert rode out to the southwest from the camp, and Michael and Thomas rode more northwest.

Michael turned to Philip and Robert. "If you catch up to us, I'll put a stake in the main trail to tell you where we started."

They knew that if they found Michael's stake, they could call it a day, because he and Thomas were ahead of them and had already checked that area. Unless, of course, they felt compelled to explore a little more.

Everyone moved slowly, studying every detail, listening intently, all of their senses on high alert. Just after noon Michael and Thomas came upon the bear massacre site. Michael dismounted and studied the signs. Thomas stayed on his horse, scanning the forest nervously. He did not like how the trees grew close together in this part of the forest. Downed trees and thick brush offered cover for an ambush. The canopy closed over their heads, letting in little light. The whole place felt vulnerable and indefensible. Thomas finally dismounted, and they walked around the area, slowly and reverently.

Thomas could not believe what he was seeing. He did not need to be an expert tracker to know what had happened there. He found a red bear print under broken fern fronds, then sat by the trail, head in his hands.

"What's wrong?" Michael asked.

Thomas did not want to talk about what was really bothering him, so he pointed at the print. "Did you see the bloody bear print here?"

Michael placed his foot beside the print and sighed tiredly. People are going to die, he thought. The print was almost exactly like the drawing James made by the campfire. If a bear this big can burst out of the woods and wipe out a hunting party of eight experienced warriors, no one was safe. Even the day camp was not safe.

He studied the area and looked up the trail. These warriors were following someone. They stopped here. Perhaps a little too close together. The bear was up there on the slope, probably behind those bushes and that big log. The bear charged down on them in a second, killing—Michael looked along the trail—killing three. Then two over there. Two more beyond them. Another fled up the trail. The bear chased, and easily caught him and his horse.

Michael scooted sideways down the steep slope. He picked up an arrow to later identify the tribe, if possible. A dead horse lay further down the hill in the dense ferns. On the trail by the pine tree were white pieces of—what is that—bone? He carefully picked through the dirt and leaves. He gingerly lifted a human foot. He looked around, frowning deeply. Another. Part of a hand. A larger bone by the horse, gnawed on with deep teeth marks. Human leg bones broken open for the marrow. His eyes widened, and he glanced briefly at Thomas. He was still sitting by the bear print, head down almost between his knees. He would wait to talk to James privately and share his suspicion that they were hunting

117

a man-eating bear. But James already suspected that from the vaquero massacre, didn't he?

He reverently laid the human bones by the dead horse. Like many Indians, he imagined that this warrior and his horse had been inseparable in life; now they would lie together in death. Maybe he and James could come back up here and bury what remains they could find.

For some reason, this scene reminded him of the massacre at the McKay plantation. The Union cavalry patrol had been given the authority to kill bushwhackers on sight, including any suspected of aiding or abetting them. On suspicion and rumor only, they had killed James and Henry's whole family. A bloody, senseless massacre. They had thrown the bodies of the dead, and those left alive, into the barn and set it on fire. Nothing left—like here.

Part of him wanted to weep at the wonton, senseless destruction, but that was not his way. For a long time, he had known or suspected what they were riding into. He also knew this new twist in the tale would not dissuade anyone from the hunt. As Robert said, they were in the dance until the music stopped.

And in a way, that was already true, although they had not encountered the bear, which would be the orchestra's main movement, leading up to the finale. He had studied classical music with Miss Alice in school. This Indian massacre would be the prelude, the opening sonata, where the moving, gliding players of this horrific dance search for each other on the dance floor of this mountain range, so aptly named Sangre de Cristo— *Blood of Christ*. Yes, indeed. Spilled blood for our sins, or someone's sins, he thought bitterly, remembering the bible lessons taught back on the McKay plantation.

He heard a slight movement and turned. Without looking at Michael, Thomas climbed onto his horse. In little more than a whisper, he said, "The sight of all these bones…reminds me of the recent war." He looked up at Michael, his face a mask of anguish. "I just need some time." Thomas turned his horse away and headed back down the hill.

Okay, Michael thought. Thomas is done for today. It wasn't much beyond noon, but they might as well head back.

On the ride back, Thomas didn't speak. Michael was comfortable with silence and knew Thomas was troubled about the war and his experiences there. At the temporary day camp, Thomas kept riding, three miles back to the herd.

"What's wrong with Thomas?" James asked.

Michael stared at Thomas' retreating back, then turned and guided James away from the others. "We came across a massacre. Looks like the bear tore up a Cheyenne hunting party."

James studied his face. "That wouldn't upset Thomas, would it?"

Michael leaned closer and whispered, "James, the bear ate eight men."

James realized his jaw was hanging down.

"Yeah." Michael turned and walked back to his horse.

James stiffened in shock. "It is a grizzly, right?" The bear definitely had to die, he thought, no matter how big and mean it was. Somehow, someway, they needed to kill it. In part of his mind, he had thought that the vaqueros' bodies had been ravaged by other animals besides the bear. No, it was just the bear that had done all that. He knew there was more to the story, but Michael was not in the mood to share it right then. He watched as Michael also rode out. Two hours later, Philip and Robert came back, and they all rode back to the herd.

The bear print did not bother Thomas. What bothered him was the carnage—parts of horses, and little bits of human flesh and bone—that slammed him back into the bloody war he worked so hard to bury and forget. He had been at Gettysburg, on Cemetery Ridge, when one hundred and seventy Confederate cannons fired for two hours to "soften up" the Union troops prior to Pickett's Charge.

Like today, he had held his head in his hands as the cannon balls rained down around them, like hail in a summer thunderstorm. The cannon balls chose whom they would take or whom they would leave behind, as indiscriminate as any other bullet on the battlefield. The sound of the cannons, the cannon balls, the screams of men and horses, had been horrific and unrelenting. He could hear it all now. See it all. Everyone around him had died, his whole platoon, including his twin brother. Some of the men were blown apart, beyond recognition. Just piles of guts and indistinguishable bones and body parts, heads with missing faces. So yes, he held his head in his hands, wept silently, and wished to God he could squeeze hard enough to eject the wretched memories out the top of his head like a spent zit.

When he arrived at the chuck wagon, without stopping his horse, he told Juan he was going out to watch the herd. And stayed out all night.

CHAPTER TEN

The next day Thomas Rhodes said he preferred to stay in camp and work on the bull horns. The group rode out after breakfast. James moved the day camp closer to the tree line to provide quicker coverage, if the need arose. Henry and Gideon stayed in the day camp, while James rode with Michael, Robert, Josiah, and Philip up to the massacre site. Two buzzards hopped off the scant remains of a dead horse and glided down the side of the mountain. The men remained quiet and reverential, but with rifles at the ready.

"This is a terrible place," Josiah whispered. "A holy place."

Philip Two Feathers nodded knowingly. This is part of the forest's sadness, he thought. But he sensed something more.

No one dismounted.

James looked all around, listening intently, sniffing the air. The others did the same. They watched their horse's ears closely. After almost ten minutes, he said, "I think it's safe to get down. Philip, would you move up the trail and keep watch?"

Philip nodded curtly and rode off.

James untied the shovel and walked to the middle of the trail, the center of the massacre. "Up here or down the slope there, by the horse?" he asked, looking a Michael.

Michael looked where James indicated. "Let's bury them by that tree. We can better tell people where it is." He was thinking of the tribe.

As James and Robert began digging, Michael deftly carved a twelve-inch circle deep into the tree bark.

Michael and Josiah began picking up the pieces they thought might have once been people, placing them reverently inside the burlap potato sack. It was slow going. When they finished, the bag was full, and James and Robert finished digging.

James did not say it, but they had done well. He was surprised at all of the bones they had found. They buried the remains quickly.

Josiah closed his eyes and raised his arms. "Be at peace, mighty warriors. Brave warriors. Go to the Great Spirit, go to your God, and be at peace in a new land. We pray you find rest for your souls, as you walk with your ancestors. Amen."

Michael also raised his arms and chanted.

Because he spent so much time with Michael growing up, James also knew Shawnee, and realized Michael's prayer was very similar to Josiah's. He was thankful that Josiah had kept his prayer simple and appropriate to the Cheyenne. James also realized Michael was keeping his voice down, speaking softly but passionately.

When Michael finished, they mounted and started up the trail toward Philip.

In the far distance, they heard gunshots.

Without comment, James spun his horse around on the narrow trail and broke into a dead run. As he flew out of the trees, he noticed that Henry and Gideon were not at the day camp. Another shot sounded in the distance. Something was happening back at the herd. Someone blew a horn.

With the others close behind, he urged the black stallion into a flat-out gallop, tail straight, ears along the head, nostrils flaring. They had to eat up three miles in a hurry. He could just see the herd. Then he heard a familiar boom—Henry's Whitworth rifle.

"I heard of them," Tells Stories said. He was an Arapaho adopted into the Ute tribe by marriage. "The Cheyenne say they shoot long—and accurate. Tried twice to take cattle."

"The Apache tried to steal horses," another added.

"What happened?" Gray Goose asked.

Tells Stories shrugged. "Some died, some ran away. No horses."

"Drovers are few during day," Gray Goose noted.

"You want cattle or just kill men?" Tells Stories asked. He could ask questions the others wouldn't, because he was married to Sleeping Wolf's sister. For the Ute, they didn't really need the cattle, or an excuse to attack. If they just killed the cattlemen that would work fine. The strangers were trespassing in the ancient Ute hunting grounds, and that was enough.

"Cattle, yes. Take scalps." Gray Goose did not like that the white people crossed their land, killed buffalo, and threatened their way of life. More came every year. In the old days, they fiercely defended their hunting territory. But over the last fifty years, more and more white people poured in, like a summer rain storm that would not end, forcing the People to make treaties, stop fighting, live in peace. It bothered him. They were warriors. Fighters for untold generations. But their territory continued to shrink, and the white men said the Ute had to live on less land every year. He did not need an excuse to kill white men.

Who were these invaders to come in here and tell them what to do? Everyone knew the answer: The invaders were the ones with the better weapons. They were the ones who came in like an army, by the hundreds. The settlers were an army. They were the ones with trained warriors protecting them, while they stole the buffalo, beaver, timber and tore up the ground. Takers. The People had lived here for thousands and thousands of years, in harmony with the land and creatures. If anything, they gave back. But not these unholy savages. They took what they wanted, and they wanted everything. The People were compelled to resist and fight them. It was the right thing to do. They still told stories and sang songs around the fire about how the U.S. Army wiped out the Cheyenne and Arapaho at Sand Creek two years before. They were in a fight for their lives with no end in sight.

The gold rush in Colorado had been hard on the Ute tribes. One treaty after another was voided to allow for the many people pouring into the territory for gold, coal and other resources. Gray Goose wanted to punish these fools, and make them pay for the pain and suffering inflicted on his people. This little group would do fine. For some reason, the cattlemen stopped before the mountains while others went into the hills. Probably hunting for gold like all greedy white men.

"Great Bear lives in those hills," Jumping Antelope said. "Cheyenne say *Vé' otsénâh kohe* dwells there— Warpath Bear, because he destroys all. Maybe they hunt." He had heard a story about the bear killing cattle people and wondered if it was true.

Gray Goose had heard the stories. "If Warpath Bear devours them, so much the better," he said bitterly. He spat into the fire for emphasis, the phlegm sizzling on a hot rock.

"How will we attack, if they shoot long?" Sleeping Wolf asked skeptically. He still thought an attack was just plain dumb. They had four good rifles but had run out of ammunition months before. The drovers looked well armed.

Gray Goose leaned forward from a seated position to lay flat on the ground, and started creeping around the fire on his belly. "Sneak closer," he hissed. "Crawl like the viper." The warriors chuckled lightly. "Watch others leave in the morning for the mountains, then kill men and take horses and cattle." He made a striking motion at Sleeping Wolf with his right hand, like a striking snake, and hissed angrily. Sleeping Wolf clutched at his throat and fell back, thrashing on the ground, and they all laughed harder.

They sat around the fire until late, discussing the details. They were experienced warriors and knew what to do.

Long before first light, they left their horses in a draw and crept toward the herd. When close, they crawled along the ground to within a stone's throw. In the early morning light, half the white men left for the mountains, and they waited.

One young man, really a boy, rode his horse out onto the prairie. He appeared to be looking for something on the ground, not paying attention to the land around him. Maybe he lost something, they thought. He rode between two braves without seeing them behind the bushes.

Sleeping Wolf looked at Gray Goose, who nodded. Gray Goose quietly followed. When beyond sight of the herd, he put an arrow in the young man's back. As he hit the ground, Gray Goose quietly ran up and took his scalp. Now that they were close to their enemy, the long rifles did not matter. He smiled wickedly: killing the others would be just as easy. He jogged the young man's horse down to the draw with their other horses.

When Gray Goose joined them, Sleeping Wolf cooed like a mourning dove: the sign to attack. They all stood, shooting arrows at the three herd guards.

The arrow slammed into the back of Emilio Rodriguez's upper left shoulder. The arrowhead glanced off the shoulder bone and stuck half way out the front of his shirt. He automatically spurred his horse, who leapt forward like a jackrabbit, as surprised as himself. The horse flew through the air, as the second arrow passed through the space between his elbow and ribs, leaving a thin slice along his left side.

Gustaf Skarsgård took his in the chest, the arrow instantly piercing his heart. One second he had been reminiscing about whaling in the South Pacific as a young man, and the next second he was already dead, slumping out of his saddle to the ground.

The arrow meant for Washington Jefferson should have killed him. But at that moment, he reached up with his left hand to swipe at an annoying blue-bottle fly, and the arrow hit his moving hand, passing completely through and viciously scraping the side of his neck, bringing an instant flow of blood. He shouted in alarm and spun his horse left, toward whomever had fired. In that instant, he decided that his own attack would be his best option, instead of continuing as a target by running away. With his right hand, he retrieved his rifle from the scabbard, chambered a round, and leveled it across his left forearm.

The Indian walked confidently toward Washington, then stopped to fire another arrow, striking Washington's horse in the upper neck just below the jaw. The horse reared, frightened by the sudden pain, and Washington's first shot went wild. But as the horse came back down, he levered another round into the chamber, stood on his toes, leaned forward in the stirrups, and shot the Indian in the chest, who expressed utter surprise as he fell back into a seated position. He could not believe the drover had fired his rifle twice in a few seconds without reloading.

"Yeah, that's a Winchester carbine!" Washington shouted. "Won it fair and square!" Someone fired off to the right. He swung his horse in that direction.

Marcus turned fourteen years old just before the cattle drive started and had been wrangler for the remuda. He had already seen combat, repelling bandits and Indians on the drive to Denver. For his reward, Robert bought him a new Henry rifle in Denver. Thomas

Rhodes was showing him how to make a bugle out of a bull's horn. There were three people out watching the little herd of cattle and the dozen remuda horses, where one might have been enough. But it was something to do.

One horse nickered and another blew, and Marcus automatically looked up. As wrangler for over four months, he had learned to understand their moods. Something was wrong. He glanced over to the herd and watched as a rider fell to the ground. Gustaf! What was going on? He jumped up, yelling, "We are under attack!" and ran for his bedroll to grab his new Henry rifle.

He kept his rifle clean and loaded at all times. He grabbed it and sprinted toward the remuda. An Indian scrambled around the edge of the milling cattle and hastily shot an arrow at him. Marcus dived forward as the arrow whipped by over his head. He rolled right, came up onto one knee, steadied the rifle and fired. The Indian stiffened and fell forward onto his face. Marcus stood, rifle at the ready, scanning the herd. Another Indian ran through the frightened herd. He fired quickly and the Indian pitched forward, but jumped up, holding his arm.

From the far right he heard a twang, and an arrow slammed into his right leg, throwing him off balance. He cried out and fell to the left. Another arrow whipped by his shoulder, but he managed to chamber a round. The Indian huffed happily, running up to him, knife in hand. Marcus tried to roll away, but the arrow had passed through his leg half way and jammed into the ground. He cried out again, but swung the rifle around, hard, like a club, hitting the Indian's legs. The warrior grunted, staggering back, but leaned forward again to dive on Marcus. Still lying on his back, Marcus leveled the rifle at the Indian's body and fired. The big bullet hit the sternum just above the heart. He landed on Marcus, coughing up a wad of blood, choking, groping for Marcus' throat. As Marcus stared at his eyes, only a few inches away, they glazed over and the grip on his throat relaxed.

Marcus pushed him off and chambered another round, then reached down and snapped off the arrow shaft sticking out the back of his leg. It hurt more than anything. He paused to catch his breath and build up his courage, panting rapidly, then deftly pulled the shaft out of his thigh in the front. He grimaced, tears falling involuntarily, but climbed haltingly to his feet. The whole front of his shirt was bloody from the Indian's mortal chest wound.

Behind him, someone fired an old dragoon. He turned to see an Indian on top of Juan Ortega, trying to knife him. Juan held both wrists, barely, shaking with the effort. Marcus took a deep breath, let it out slow, and fired. The Indian slumped onto Juan, a small dark hole in his ribs on the right side. Still lying there, Juan turned his head to the left and nodded to Marcus. He had been stabbed twice, in the arm and chest, but not deep wounds. Someone fired from the other side of the herd. Marcus thought it must be Thomas Rhodes or O'Keefe.

Six Indians were on remuda horses, trying to get the cattle running northeast. Marcus heard a buzzing sound, like a wasp, pass close overhead followed by a distant boom. One of the six Indians slid off his horse, already dead. Marcus had to grin, remembering how he and the others had hid behind the rock wall on the McKay plantation while Uncle Billy and Mr. McKay shot over them with the Wentworth sharpshooter rifles. The hexagon bullet made a peculiar sound, like an angry bee as it flew by. Already, he felt better. With James or Henry firing, the others could not be far behind, and the Indians would be driven off.

A shot on the other side of the cattle made Marcus swing around. Two Indians on the south side of the herd were shooting toward the wagon: one had Gustaf's rifle.

O'Keefe had been sleeping and was up on one knee, firing his pistol.

J.C. Graves

CHAPTER ELEVEN

When Henry heard the shots back at the herd, he grabbed his gear and jumped on his horse. "Come on Gideon, the boys are under attack."

They raced as fast as the horses could run, but three miles was a long way to travel in an emergency. The shots increased.

Two hundred yards from the wagon, Henry spotted a tall prairie dog mound. "Keep riding!" he shouted at Gideon, "But don't get between me and the herd."

Henry pulled out the ramrod and laid it next to the paper cartridges and firing caps, deftly inserting a cap on the nipple. The rifle was ready to fire. He spotted six Indians on horseback, moving the cattle away from the wagon. He lined up and fired. An Indian flew off a horse. Henry sat up to reload then reacquired his sight picture. "Three," he whispered to himself, and another Indian flew left off his horse.

As a McKay Ranger, they always prepared to fire when James said, *On three.* Then actually fired a second later, with the word *three.* He could load fast, because he opened the cartridge paper with his teeth, and jammed the paper and powder into the barrel at the same time. Then he started the hexagon bullet with his palm, and rammed it into place with the rod, usually only one time. When he laid the ramrod on the ground, he automatically picked up a firing cap—no wasted motion. Through practice and experience, all of his moves were quick and accurate. Like his shooting.

He reloaded in eight seconds and lay back down, scanning left and right. There! An Indian running through the brush, charging in from the left. But just as he was about to tap the front trigger, Gideon moved his running horse in front of Henry's line of fire, and he growled under his breath. He swung the rifle back to the right. There! Another Indian on a remuda horse, trying to move the cattle. He fired and quickly reloaded.

Gideon rode right up to the chuck wagon, firing his rifle at an Indian among the cattle. He wasn't sure if he hit him, because he seemed to fall and scurry away.

O'Keefe stood up from behind the wagon wheel. "Could sure use some help!" he shouted.

Gideon spurred his horse around the wagon, moving toward the remuda. An Indian on O'Keefe's left and behind him, stood, drawing back the bow string.

Henry saw the Indian draw down on O'Keefe and quickly swung over and fired. The Indian spun around, but O'Keefe went to the ground. He heard horses approaching from behind. That would be James, he thought. He scooped up the cartridges and firing caps tin, and mounted his horse.

Henry pulled the Winchester out of the front scabbard on the right and dropped the Wentworth rifle into its long scabbard behind the saddle on the left. As he spurred the horse, he chambered a round. A shot from behind made him look around. The others were closing quickly; James held both revolvers. He returned the Henry rifle to the scabbard and also pulled both revolvers, turning his horse a little right with his right knee. He flew past the chuck wagon, as James streaked by the other side on his fearless black stallion. They swept through the camp, revolvers out, firing left and right, riding straight into the little herd.

The Indians on the horses shouted and tried to ride away, but James and Henry had the momentum and chased them down. James trampled a running Indian with his stallion. Three Indians were afoot among the cattle. They shot arrows, one taking Henry's hat off. For one full minute, arrows and bullets filled the air. James stood in the stirrups to shoot two fleeing Indians. He shot one and Thomas shot the other from off to the left. Henry pulled up. Two arrows stuck out of his bedroll behind the saddle: one from the left, one from the right. He had been moving too fast for them.

James continued until he was sure there were no other Indians down that way beyond the herd, then circled back around, studying every bush and rock, his Henry rifle at the ready. He found another Indian hiding behind a small boulder. The Indian stood, hands raised, and James shot him in the forehead. "We are *not* the U.S. Cavalry," he whispered, "And we do *not* take prisoners." Another Indian jumped up and ran north. James turned his horse to the right, stood high in the stirrups and prepared to fire, but Washington Jefferson shot the Indian, who fell forward in a cloud of dust. James nodded to him, and circled the herd and the camp twice to be sure they didn't miss any others, then rode in.

Behind a clump of bushes, he spotted someone on the ground, the boots sticking out. Wizzy lay face down, an arrow in his back, and part of his scalp missing. James shook his head, feeling a deep sadness descend like a cloud. The poor boy, he thought. Just getting started, just figuring out what path to take, and now this miserable, wretched end. He dismounted, deftly pulled out the arrow, and rolled the body over, so he could pick him up.

Through half-opened eyes, Wizzy whispered, "Mr. McKay, I don't feel so good."

"Hold on, boy," James said hoarsely, "We'll get you some help, pronto."

He hoisted Wizzy up onto his saddle, then climbed up behind him. They raced straight down to the wagon, scattering the cattle. "Need help here!" he shouted, sliding to a stop. Everyone gathered around to ease Wizzy off the horse.

"On that blanket—put in back of wagon," Juan said, taking control. "Careful." He shook off Whipple, who was trying to bind up his knife wounds. "Whipple, put water on to boil. Wait." He spun around to James. "Find missing piece of scalp!" he shouted loudly, although only six feet away.

James whistled loudly and called for everyone to gather. "We need to find Wizzy's missing scalp. It must be on one of the Indians. Find it. Hurry!" He hoped the Indian that scalped the lad was among the dead and hadn't escaped.

Everyone scattered. In less than two minutes, from out beyond the remuda, Henry yelled, "Found it!"

He rushed in and handed the bloody mass to Juan.

Juan worked on Wizzy for almost three hours with Henry and Josiah standing by to hold him, if necessary. He carefully cleaned the skull and scalp. The skull continued to weep blood, as he aligned the missing piece properly and carefully placed a horse hair stitch every quarter inch. Fortunately, Wizzy never moved until the very end.

"Oh, it hurts, it hurts, it hurts," he moaned over and over, twisting and turning.

"Hold him still," Juan said softly. "Almost done."

Juan finished the scalp, bound the head tightly, and turned Wizzy over. He probed the back with his fingers. The arrow broke an upper rib and entered six inches, but didn't hit any vital organs. Juan cleaned the wound liberally with iodine and wrapped him up tight.

When they turned him over, Wizzy moaned louder and tried to rise, eyes fluttering. Josiah helped him sit up. Juan poured a double shot of the new Tennessee bourbon and held it to his lips.

"Sí, muy malo. You no like, but help," he promised soothingly. Wizzy winced and choked up half of the unfamiliar liquid. He had never had anything stronger than beer, and only two of those in his sixteen years. Juan turned to Henry. "Keep Wizzy from scratching head."

Michael, Philip and Robert returned to camp with a string of ten Indian horses and Wizzy's. Marcus and James met them by the herd, and Marcus took the horses.

"Ute." Michael said. "Looks like maybe twelve or so got away, mostly wounded."

Robert said, "They gave as good as they got."

James nodded in agreement and looked off across the prairie. It was a beautiful day: soft westerly breeze, fat white clouds drifting east, a small herd of pronghorns grazing nearby, several of the curious creatures watched them carefully. Apparently, the gunshots did not bother them. He wondered about that. Part of him wished he could see the Indians riding away, so he could go after them. But maybe not. "Well, that's probably the last we'll see of any Indians."

Robert put his hand on James' shoulder. "Because word will spread to leave us alone. You and Henry did fine. Mighty fine." He had seen their fearlessness in the face of battle before. It would not work well to be their enemy. And you could scarcely find more faithful and loyal friends.

Philip and Josiah began dragging the Indian bodies off to the dry gulch two hundred feet northeast of the camp. Around the fire, Juan and Whipple tended to the other wounded.

143

"Need iodine," Juan said to Robert.

O'Keefe took an arrow to the upper left arm, but it passed completely through. Juan cleaned out Marcus' leg wound and tied it up tight. Marcus put on a brave face, but could not stop a few tears from leaking out. In a private contest, Emilio and Washington Jefferson stared intently into each other's eyes, never blinking or acknowledging the stinging iodine as Juan tended to their deep scratch wounds. Washington had great welts across his back from his time as a slave, but this wound was the only one in a straight line—left to right. Whipple had a cut chin from falling out of the wagon in his panic. Henry took an arrow to the boot, but it only scratched his ankle. He didn't even know it was there, broken off, until someone said something. Thomas Rhodes was shot with Gustaf's Spencer rifle, but the bullet only grazed his head above the right ear. He looked terrible; his right shoulder bloody. But he refused Juan's advances, tightly tying his own bandana around his head.

Henry and Gideon carried Gustaf's body over to the fire.

"I'm going to miss his whaling stories," Henry lamented.

"He sure loved the sea," Michael said.

Thomas limped over to Gustaf's blanket roll and brought it over. "He don't have much," he said, laying it down by the fire.

"Why are you limping?" James asked.

"Don't ask," Thomas said testily.

James' right eyebrow arched up.

"Okay then!" he shouted. "By the Lord Almighty and the muddy Mississippi, I got a Robert Garcia Preston wound. You satisfied?"

Robert stood over at the wagon, dipping water out of the bucket for a drink. "You got a what?"

Thomas glared at him and James for a few seconds, then dropped his pants and slowly turned in a circle. Around his waist was a white cloth, resembling one of his favorite shirts, that held a wadded-up bandage on his right butt cheek, also a match for his Sunday-go-to-meeting shirt. "Just a scratch, and I don't need old Juan nursing my backside and cooing over my injuries like the old nursemaid he is." He pulled up his pants, glaring at everyone.

Juan chortled, saying something in Spanish under his breath, while Whipple tended his wounds.

James let a smile briefly cross his face and looked at Henry. Henry was not trying to hide his merriment, smiling from ear to ear.

Robert said, "I think I resent that remark, Thomas. It's kinda mean-spirited and hurts my feelin's."

O'Keefe laughed at Robert. "Well, it's true, darlin', if'n you think about it," he said, also smiling broadly.

"What do you have there?" James asked Henry.

Henry carefully opened Gustaf's gear. The men gathered closer, Thomas nudging Robert.

"Look at that," Henry said. "I think it's a Swedish bible."

"Really?" Robert asked, reaching. Henry handed it to James, who handed the book to Robert. "Never noticed him readin' it."

"I think he read it when out watching the cattle; you know, during the day," James said.

"Saw him reading it by full moonlight one time," Josiah said.

"He recited the 23rd Psalm for me—in Swedish," Marcus said. "You could tell it was the 23rd Psalm just by the way he said it."

James turned to Robert. "Do you know where he hails from?"

"When he signed up, he listed no kin of any kind; I asked twice."

"Might have come over from Sweden by himself," Gideon offered.

James shook his head. "Too bad. Someone, somewhere is going to wonder what ever happened to him."

Henry took the bible back from Robert. "Lots of fellows out here in the West with different names, mysterious pasts, and those who don't want to be found." He was remembering his investigation of the stage holdup and the search for the killer, who turned out to be in the trail drive to Denver under an alias.

Gideon added, "And some folks just don't have kin anywhere."

Robert pulled two wayward arrows out of cows. They were only lightly wounded and would recover easily. One of the remuda horses had caught a stray bullet just below the ear and had to be put down. Juan doctored Washington Jefferson's horse and assured him that it would recover quickly. "Better," Washington said, patting the horse affectionately. "The old boy saved my life, catching that arrow meant for me."

James untied the shovel behind his saddle and started digging by an old scrub pine and rocks. The sun would set in two hours. Gideon joined him with the other shovel. Soon others came over and helped dig. Four of the men lowered Gustaf into the grave and carefully placed his jacket over his face. Josiah Bell said words over him and they sang *Amazing Grace,* then everyone helped shovel in the dirt. Rhodes carved a cross with Gustaf's name on it and the date—June 1866, and pounded it into the ground, as the sun dipped below the horizon.

Josiah finished with, "And may ye have square sails and fair winds with following seas. Amen."

Everyone said amen.

William O'Keefe added softly, hat in hand, "Aye, and a soft wind at your back, laddie."

Everyone said amen, again.

Marcus wiped his eyes and quietly asked his brother, "Josiah, what is a following sea?"

"The waves coming directly at you from astern, I mean from behind. Helps you get to your destination better, quicker."

"Where did you learn that?"

"From reading *Moby Dick* and then talking to Gustaf about what some of the nautical terms meant. He was a whaler in his other life, you know—harpooner actually. Loved to talk about his adventures, if someone would ask."

"Can I read the book when you're done?"

"Of course, then we can talk about it." He put his arm around Marcus' shoulders, pulling him close. "I can tell you what I learned from him."

Juan told everyone how Marcus saved him, and Marcus thanked Robert again for the Henry rifle, noting that he was able to fire quicker when needed, which had saved his life and Juan's.

Now fully awake, Wizzy struggled with debilitating pain, the worse he had ever experienced. He lay under the wagon on a makeshift cot, where Juan could keep a closer eye on him. He moaned for hours, tossing and turning in the blankets, panting and sweating. Occasionally, he would try to rub the throbbing, painful wound on his head, and the blood would start oozing through the stitches. Juan rebuked him and threatened to hog tie him if he didn't stop. Through clenched jaw and eyes, Wizzy complained that the pain persisted without let up. Juan would only give him a shot of bourbon every few hours, which Wizzy learned to hungrily swallow quickly and easily.

When Henry visited him, he pleaded through teary eyes, "If I die, bury me in those hills out yonder. Put my name on a wooden plaque, so's I'm not forgotten or somethin'." He trembled uncontrollably.

"You aren't going to die, dear Wizzy," Henry assured him, kneeling down beside the cot, rocking his shoulder affectionately. "I know it's hard, believe me, but you'll get through this."

"It hurts mighty powerful, Mr. Henry. Won't let up none."

"It will pass."

Juan mouthed, *Fever.* Henry nodded.

"My real name's Wisdom Anderson."

"Wisdom?"

"Ma named me. Next brother up is Solomon. You get the idea."

"A bible theme, of sorts." Henry dabbed his sweaty forehead with a cool, damp cloth.

"Yeah, from the bible. Took some teasin' over it." As Wizzy spoke, he kept his eyes tightly closed.

"Okay, Mr. Wisdom Anderson. I'll put your proper name on the plaque should you give up the ghost, but it's not likely to happen today." He grinned, playfully shaking Wizzy's shoulder again, but the young man was sweating in pain and moaned through clenched teeth.

"Here's something to think about. Someday, you're going to have one great story to tell around the campfire, to your children and grand-children, as long as you shall live." He held Wizzy's hand, which suddenly gripped his tightly.

"Oh…I don't know," he panted.

Henry squeezed is shoulder. "There I was, you might begin. Surrounded by wild hostiles. You will tell the wide-eyed children at your knees, I fought them to a standstill, guns blazing, lead bullets flying; but somehow, I stood my ground against the onslaught. Their wild calls only inflamed my vigor and will to live. I needed neither water nor sustenance for seven days. On the final attack, six thousand of my worthy adversaries on horseback charged over the hill…"

"Six thousand!" Wizzy choked out in disbelief.

"Okay. Let me see. On the final attack at the very break of dawn, six hundred of my worthy enemies charged over the hill with barbaric blood-curdling screams, overwhelming our simple fortifications. Nevertheless, I laughed and displayed my long Bowie knife, given to me by none other than Jim Bowie himself, and charged into the fray, whipping that Roman short sword left and right. I piled my noble victims around me, covered in their red blood as if I'd bathed in the same. And still they came, ignoring certain death and dismemberment.

"My blade sang among them, slicing and carving, until a wretched cowardly dog stood on the pile of dead bodies, nearly twenty feet high, and shot me with an arrow. In my back! In my back! In my momentary confusion, they rushed en masse, and darkness descended. They shouted with wicked glee at their enemy's humiliation. The chief amongst them reached into the melee and tore my scalp from my head with knife and fist. I passed out, believing my days of walking the earth had come to an abrupt end.

"But. Then. The sound of a loud trumpet met my fading ears. At first, I thought it was that famous angel Gabriel, that distinguished and eminent biblical messenger, sent to retrieve my battered soul for my heavenly reward. But no! Alas, twas the intrepid U.S. Cavalry descended upon this historic scene of darkness, gloom and despair, destroying the last of my bitter enemies, except those as had slunk away like the vermin they were.

"As the cavalrymen gathered around, hats in respectful hands, to their utter shock and amazement, I moved! I still breathed. My heart still beat. With mythological skill, a dexterous U.S. Army doctor took a patch of hair off my chest and attached it to my head, which you can see and touch, noting the horrific scar surrounding the site of the torture. The joyful men hoisted me on their shoulders, cheering and shouting praises. Never the like had been seen before, and never since to this day."

Henry tenderly touched Wizzy's forehead, wiping the beaded sweat away. The boy had fallen asleep, his face peaceful. Then began a slow clap by someone, followed by more clapping and then cheering. He looked up, surprised.

James stood, bowing with flourishes. "Hail to Wizzy, Knight of the Cattle Drive, King of Slayers, Bane of Red Skins everywhere!"

Robert waved him over. "Come over here to the fire, Henry, Master Story Teller, and regale us with more tales of splendor and might against impossible odds."

O'Keefe asked, "Aye, and would you be able to add in some fair lassie, who might be needin' a rescue or savin' by the hero of this story?" Secretly, O'Keefe was stunned at the tale, so easily told, that it flowed off Henry's tongue as if he were a first-account witness, watching from a hidden place or bluff overlooking the epic battle. He always thought of himself as a better-than-average story teller. Now he would have to do some preparation before he shared another tall tale. He finally had some honest competition.

J.C. Graves

CHAPTER TWELVE

Everyone else had turned in; Robert sat with James by the fire. "Want to call off this here bear hunt?" "Been thinking on just that," James admitted.

They didn't speak for a long time. Robert poured more coffee for them both. "That's the last of it." He set the empty blackened coffee pot to the side.

"Let's see," James began, "Among the uninjured, we have Henry, Gideon, Josiah, Michael, Philip, you and me. That's seven." James carefully sipped the scalding hot coffee. The coffee was from breakfast: old, black, and thick as tar, strong and bitter, and fit his mood perfectly. "We can continue with that many if we move the herd closer to the mountains, where we have the day camp. Keep closer together."

Robert nodded. Being spread out with two camps had lured the Indians, an easy conquest—to them. He figured it was his mistake and a poor decision based on a possible threat from the bear. Well, to hades with the varmint. "Let's move the herd a little north of your day camp today, actually." He did not want to go home and have Pablo accuse them of cowardice or quitting in the face of these obstacles. They would just have to see this through, although he and James carried major doubts. Pride and honor were driving the train now. He was used to taking orders and giving them. James the same. In effect, they had given orders to themselves, damn the consequences.

The next day they moved the cattle to a spot a few miles north of their last day camp and much closer to the mountain range. James sat his horse, studying the wood line. He worried that the trees started only fifty yards away. If running hard, the bear could cover that distance quickly. How quickly? He frowned, thinking about what that might look like. As fast as he could load and fire — ten or twelve seconds average now; he might not get off a second shot. Even if all four of them shot the bear with their high-caliber sharpshooter rifles, a creature that big, that angry…no, they would not stop it before it killed someone, maybe everyone. A sobering thought. He frowned, considering that chilling scenario happening at three in the morning. On a very dark and rainy night. No light. The bear charging through the cattle, then among the sleeping men, wreaking havoc and slaughtering people like the big saw at the lumber mill. Instead of saw dust and wood chips flying, it would be bone and sinew and blood accompanied by desperate, horrific screams.

James never considered shooting the bear with just the 44-caliber Henry rifle, even if he could fire sixteen rounds or more per minute. The Whitworth round was 45-caliber, but moving at what he considered twice the speed, although he did not know how to measure something like that. When it hit the bear, the damage should be profound. He hoped. If he was able, his first shot would be with the famous hexagon Whitworth bullet, then grab the Henry and fire as quickly as he could chamber rounds. All head shots. No use guessing where the heart might be on a creature that big. He would aim for that special sweet spot between the eyes.

He frowned. Yeah, that's right, he thought, if he could see the beast clearly. All of his detailed planning came to naught if the bear dove into them in the dark of night, and he could not see what he was firing at. He looked around at the fire. They could gather extra wood and keep the fire going strong, even in a rain, if that was possible. Some of the storms could dump gallons of water in a short time. With their backs to the fire, the bear would have to come to them. Perhaps in that light, they could mass their fires on the beast in a night attack. If they were ready.

He remembered the Indian massacre up on the mountain trail. One thing was true, they could not all be bunched up together in the defense. In a few seconds, the bear could tear them apart. But if they spread out, while one reloaded, the other could fire, then another, then another. They would need fighting positions, trenches surrounding a kill zone. Yes, that would work—might work, if they could get the bear out onto the flat below the tree line. Maybe using a cow or two. What might the bear do? Attack the position down the middle, or starting on the far left or far right? If the bear attacked their flank, it might roll them up, charging around the outside of their ambush area, using their own dug defensive positions to its advantage. Lots of "ifs." Too many? He brushed an annoying fly away from his face. Was he giving the bear too much credit? Was he giving it human intelligence?

In a way, he had come to respect the bear as an honorable adversary. He did not think of it as an animal to be simply hunted, killed and stuffed as a trophy. No. This was like fighting a Union general, who knew the terrain intimately, knew the country, could see in the dark, could sniff out his enemy, and destroy him mercilessly with tooth and claw. General Warpath Bear. *Sir, General Warpath Bear is attacking the northern flank, should I deploy the troops?* James smiled to think how Henry and the others would react to this admission, to this outlandish image. Michael wouldn't laugh.

Gideon took charge of setting up the bear ambush. He determined where to stake the bait cow, then marked the fighting positions. People not involved in scouting, look out, or guarding the herd, helped dig.

It had been two days since the Indian attack. Because there were only two shovels and a pick, Gideon, Robert and Whipple were the only ones digging shallow fighting positions. Wizzy could not stand laying around the wagon and sat on the ground nearby, watching. The wound in his back was healing nicely, and his scalp pain had subsided to almost nothing. Mostly it itched on occasion, which everyone said was good. Ortega had bandaged it tightly and warned him to relax and let his body heal.

The day was hot and cloudless. After an hour, Henry spelled Whipple. While sitting there, Wizzy took off his shirt, his bright white back facing to the south and the full glare of the sun. Henry started to say something, then kept his peace. The boy has to learn, he thought. He would be burnt in an hour. Although he was only two years older than Wizzy, it seemed he had lived a lifetime in the last two years. Killing Union soldiers and outlaws as a ranger had hardened him some. But when Mr. Cooper set up his capture and beating, the last remnants of his boyhood had vanished, savagely crushed out of him. The McKay Rangers had been hard on the Union troops, killing the officers and sergeants of those units that tried to terrorize the Asheville area. So, the troopers took out their frustration on his body, beating and kicking him unconscious, mashing his nose, while leading him up to Death's Doorstep—but not quite through. He had struggled back to normalcy. His body had been broken, but also part of himself, inside. They had beaten the childhood out of him.

When they fled North Carolina to escape the bounty that remained on each of them after the war, he had taken command of one of the groups, leading the three wagons of families down to Charleston, then Savannah, and then off to Texas. Through months of trial and fire, he had grown in years. Just before they arrived in Mobile, Alabama, he and Josiah and Michael stopped a train robbery. Noting Henry's quality and how he seemed older than his years, Marshal Tibbits made him a Deputy U.S. Marshal to help escort the notorious Gil

Branch to another town for trial. Then once in Texas, Judge Hornby hired him to solve a Wells Fargo stage robbery.

In the western frontier, where law and order could be a sketchy proposition in places, a person's age was not so important as the quality of their life and reputation. Henry looked a little salty with his scars and broken nose. But there was a certain look about his eyes that gave people pause. More than one hombre, looking for a fight, hesitated at those eyes—an empty blue-green that seemed to look right through you. Those eyes said, *I've seen your kind before.* Not a haughty contempt that dared a fight, but a knowing measure and understanding of a person's soul. A look he shared with James, although James' eyes seemed more menacing when riled.

When they were younger, people said they looked enough to be twins. Now that Henry had had his face reshaped a few times, the one thing they still shared were the cool gazing hazel eyes. But where James was always serious and seldom smiled, Henry flashed a quick and ready smile with little provocation.

Wizzy had been amazed to learn that Henry was only a few years older than him. Wizzy had joined up with outlaws after leaving home and had been trying to act like a real tough man. Robert hired them in the last month of the drive to help with the herd. To Wizzy, Henry seemed much older — acted older, talked older — in all the ways that mattered. When Wizzy left the outlaws to stay with the herd and return to Texas, his goal was to emulate Henry, be Henry, so he watched him closely, seldom out of his sight. In a sense, he felt like Henry was his older brother. He saw Henry as he imagined himself one day.

After another hour of digging, Henry turned to Wizzy and sent him to lie down in the wagon. It was not a request and Wizzy knew it. Reluctantly, he put his shirt on and flinched, noticing how much his back hurt from the raw sunburn. Henry smiled to see it.

James walked into the center of the ambush area and used a stick to draw a big circle in the soil. "We'll put a stack of wood here," he said.

"'I'll get one of Ortega's tarps, so we can fill it with wood and buffalo chips," Gideon said.

James pointed. "Up the ridge behind that white rock is a lightning struck tree. I think two horses could pull the bigger pieces down here."

"I'll do that," Emilio volunteered and walked to his horse.

James scanned the ridge, wondering how much wood they would really need.

As if sensing his thoughts, Gideon said, "I'll have Emilio bring in wood until we have a month's supply."

"We will probably need enough to keep a big fire going all night in the rain. Think that way and you'll gather enough."

Great Bear awoke in the dark—long before sunrise—unrested, irritable, confused. He slowly rose to his feet, shakily at first, and walked to the cave entrance. The full moon showed through the trees. His vision wavered briefly, a disorienting feeling that made him tremble. The image of the white moon seemed to stretch, as if pulled from below, then from the right side, then the left. A rainbow of colors flashed across his vision. He shook his head in irritation. The persistent ache in his head never left but somehow seemed worse this morning. He sniffed the ground and stood on his hind legs, probing and sniffing the air. What was that smell? It seemed vaguely familiar, but he could not quite recall what it was. Was it the scent of a female who wanted him? He turned, sniffing. Off to the left. His chest rumbled. The scent felt like she was calling to him, drawing him forward. He could not resist.

He walked to the north. Moonlight finally gave way to long morning shadows then bright sunlight. The direct light bothered him for a long time, and he walked along with his right eye closed against the morning sun's brightness, staying in the forest and shade of the trees. He plodded ahead, driven by a vague instinct and little else. At times the elusive scent disappeared, but he stubbornly continued, wagging his great head left and right, his nose automatically sampling the air currents. Female grizzlies never attracted him before, but now he felt compelled to seek her.

In late morning, with a shift in the wind, the scent suddenly grew stronger. He stood on a ridge, turning left and right. Far down in the valley below, he spotted a mother grizzly and cub trotting quickly away. At some level, he wondered if they were running away from him. His anger swelled and he huffed loudly, the sound carrying down the slope. He scrapped the ground in fury, clods of dirt flying, and charged down the hill to kill them.

The old female sow stopped abruptly and spun around, emitting a pathetic cry. Far up the ridge she could see Great Bear, the huge boar stood tall and threatening. Long ago she had seen him and knew he was *different*. But also dangerous. Over the years, she had had many cubs. She felt very protective and had maimed aggressive male grizzlies before. But not this unusual bear. If he wanted, he could kill her and the cub without hesitation. Suddenly Great Bear bound down the steep slope, galloping toward them. Fear swept over her like a cold wave of water. She barked at her son and broke into a full out run.

The day before she and her cub had passed through the Sangre de Cristo mountains, but on the west side. When she found the Great Bear scat, she shook with fear. Something about the scat was wrong: a lingering sense of humans, but also anguish and fear and dark malice. She knew instinctively that her cub was in danger, perhaps herself. Her home range was to the north, so she set a furious pace, her one-year-old struggling to keep up. Despite her desperate dash for safety, the big bear was here. Palpable fear drove her forward. The fact that the great bear had found them and now gave chase, must mean he meant to kill them.

She could have easily outrun Great Bear, but the cub cried pitifully when she began to pull away. What to do? If they reached the river…she turned sharply west without looking back. At this point the river was not wide or deep, and they plunged in. The cub started to cross, but she growled at him and turned to run and swim with the current to the southwest. They swam then scrambled along sand bars, gravel spits, boulders and logs, then swam again, always desperate to get away.

She looked back. Nothing. Had they fooled the great bear or outrun him? Her panic began to ease a little and she slowed, so her little one could keep up easier and catch his breath. Still, she continued, looking back as much as forward. She did not know how far they had run, walking and running, swimming often, then walking again. Her little one was done in and falling behind, mewing miserably. She kept slowing until they were barely walking along. Have they gone far enough? Was it safe? She stopped on a sandbar and sat heavily. Her cub dropped his head into her lap, panting and exhausted, eyes tightly closed, tongue half out.

They had been moving quickly for almost eight miles. As the fear that drove their exhausting journey began to fade, she let her eyes droop. The sun felt good on her face. A bee buzzed by her head. A black fly landed at the corner of her left eye. She shook her head and opened her eyes. She gave an involuntary start. Her cub groaned at the sudden movement but kept sleeping, a light snore coming from his open mouth.

On the bank, not more than thirty feet away, the giant bear stood, studying her. Some instinctive sense deep in her heart, warned that if she ran, he would catch and kill them both. So, she sat, frozen, breath coming in rapid, shallow pants. The cub nestled deeper into her warm stomach fur, unaware of their precarious situation.

CHAPTER THIRTEEN

A t the sight of the old sow running away, Great Bear ran down the slope then broke into an easy trot. He lost sight of his quarry and slowed. He found where the female turned to the river. In some deep part of his wounded brain, he remembered enjoying these types of games. Chase. Hiding. Seeking. Something different from the ordinary and routine life he led. He found where they plunged into the river but the trail did not continue on the far side. He looked left, then right. His ears twitched. Left. He walked along the bank. He did not need to see them; he could hear the distant splashing, as they swam and ran down the river. Trees and brush choked the river bank, but he took his time, wandering through various trails, or temporarily swinging away from the river, to work his way back when able.

For over two hours he plodded along. Finally, he crawled his way past an old willow tree and river debris, and spotted them sitting on a sandbar in the middle of the river. The run had been fun. He could not remember why he had chased them. During the chase, the reason had evaporated with a shift in the wind. The mother grizzly noticed him and did not move, but he felt no emotion, no sense of family or connection or need. She could have been a stump or boulder for all he cared; it just didn't matter anymore.

For his size, he was surprisingly quiet. He stood, watching them for a few minutes, when a distant sound caused him to turn to the left, looking down the river. He dropped to all fours and walked slowly in that direction, a growing edge in his mind. Like a bee sting. A sense of annoyance and rage bubbled just beneath the surface, threatening to erupt.

Marty Walker and Son Hu Wang had been panning for gold along that stretch of the river since before the snow melted. Marty looked the typical prospector: faded canvas pants with frayed rope suspenders; dirty long underwear that he wore year-round in all weather; a floppy, nondescript hat with various holes and snags; and long scraggly black hair generously sprinkled with gray. He hadn't shaved since the beginning of spring, and his straggly, salt-and-pepper beard had never been groomed. His eyesight was excellent, but the eyes floated—a little rheumy—given his suffering from seasonal allergies due to the many grasses on the prairie, although he did not know what allergies were. His face was dark tanned and deeply wrinkled from a life outdoors under the sun, but otherwise unmarked. He had a pair of old army boots that had never seen polish, inherited from a dead man he stumbled upon after an Indian massacre on a homestead. When in the stream, he left the boots on the bank. He had never owned socks. In fact, since it was just him and Wang, that day he worked in his long underwear, the legs rolled up past his knees. The water was bitter cold, but he was used to it and not given to complaint, especially with the rewards at hand.

The year before, they had met in a gold camp up in the Rockies. Marty hired Wang to help and they became friends. Wang was a typical Chinese gold prospector, lured to the United States by the promise of wealth, when all anyone wanted was his strong back. Many of his relatives went off to work the railroad, but he found work in various gold prospecting and mining communities, quietly filling little bags of gold dust. He never had quite enough to call himself prosperous. His brother, Chan, opened a laundry, married, and did well. But Wang always wanted more.

His Chinese linen clothes soon wore out. Although he kept his long, braided hair, he dressed in the more durable clothes of the typical prospector, except for his straw, hand-woven, wide-brimmed coolie hat. He was almost half the size of Marty and dressed about the same. But where Marty never washed, Wang bathed daily. Where Marty never groomed, Wang washed his hair, combed it out, braided it fresh, shaved the few hairs that grew on his face, and even took care of his teeth with a pig's hair toothbrush he brought from China. Although opposites in almost every respect besides clothing, they were fast and true friends.

Marty thought the best part of their friendship was Wang's cooking. He had a knack for finding wild things, like mushrooms and onions and spices. Together with trout and the occasional deer, pronghorn sheep or mountain goat, they did well for themselves, and seldom went to town except for meager supplies, like coffee, tea, sugar, dried fruit, flour, salt, and powder and shot.

The four large tin cans—eighty pounds each—buried behind the small army surplus tent held three-hundred and twenty pounds of gold dust and nuggets. They did not want to take it all in to the assayer until the plot was played out. If they went too early, every yahoo and scoundrel would discover their claim. The next thing you know, hundreds of prospectors would be working the river right alongside them, ruining their chances to get rich, or trying to rob them — most likely the later. This time they would go all the way to Denver, cash out, and retire.

Just two weeks before, they had cut back the river bank and found the extension of a wide and ancient seam in the bedrock, and they were no longer grubbing up dust and the occasional nugget with their pans and sluice box. No siree. Instead, nuggets the size of Wang's little finger filled the crack, scattered throughout. Marty figured they could work this area until the end of summer and retire for the rest of their lives. Actually, he knew that greed kept him at it, because they had enough to retire on now, if they lived simply. But as long as the river continued to give up her riches, he felt duty bound and morally obligated to relieve her of the buried treasure.

At fifty-two years old, he knew his days of living off the land while performing back-breaking work were coming to an end. He had struck it rich twice before and lost it all. The first fortune slipped through his fingers because he was young and stupid, or so he reasoned. At twenty-five, with fifteen thousand dollars in his pocket, he could not spend it fast enough on women, booze, and gambling. Suddenly, he had lots of friends with their hands out, or in his pockets, and the money was gone in less than two months.

The second fortune, when he was forty-one, came from a Nevada silver mine. Careful as he was, made wise through some trial and more error, he still lost most of it to a mining company with lots of lawyers. A day later, he was robbed of the remainder in an alley and left for dead. Rich beyond measure one day and dead broke the next—a lump on his head the size of a chicken egg for his troubles.

No, this time would be different. He and Wang would get a nice house in town with a housekeeper to do the chores. They would sit on the front porch in rocking chairs, smoke nice cigars, and play checkers or dominoes, and every night they would walk down to the saloon for a refreshing drink. A simple life, the merits of which they discussed almost every evening. The housekeeper would cook, but Wang would indulge himself at the stove when the desire hit him. He had a knack for stews and pies, and Marty would heartily encourage his efforts in that arena.

Wang said, "Give housekeeper Sunday off. Me cook. Mushroom beef stew, you like. Fresh biscuits, lots of butter. Apple pie with cinnamon."

174

"Sounds like a plan," Marty replied, rubbing his stomach eagerly. "A mighty fine plan. And I will eat all your mistakes."

"Mistakes! What mistakes?" He held up his little fist and shook it threateningly. "I cook good food. Best food. You like. Get fat, lazy. Like tick on dog."

No matter how mad he made Wang, they always laughed in the end. Wang's singsong rebuke made Marty's eyes twinkle mischievously, so he baited the poor fellow mercilessly. And Wang had to smile, his madness an act and show for their mutual enjoyment.

They did not worry about gold dust anymore. Marty hummed *Camp Town Races*, as he worked, shoveling gravel and black sand into the ten-foot-long sluice box, while Wang cheerfully and deftly plucked nuggets out of the riffles. Neither heard the approaching bear over the sound of the river water, spilling around rocks, and the persistent scoop of the shovel.

For all his enormous size, Great Bear walked along silently. The pads on his long feet were calloused, like all animals, but more sensitive than most. He had a way of rolling his feet along, brushing away debris like dry leaves, sticks and twigs, so his passing was mostly soundless, even when he walked beside a trail instead of directly on it.

When he saw the miners, he lowered his head, red eyes blazing, but he kept walking. Quietly. Purposefully. He walked right up to the men. As his shadow crossed the sluice box, they both looked up, startled—and died. Great Bear's right paw flew up in a lightning quick swipe and the eight-inch claws caused Marty's head to plop into the river, drifting away downstream. Wang's neck was cut nearly through, the head flopping onto his back, held by the spinal cord.

The larger man's body caught the current and floated down the river, spinning peacefully, his life blood reddening the water around him. But the smaller man's body slumped over the wooden contraption. Great Bear settled down next to the body and ate everything except the clothes. He crushed the skull in his jaws and licked out the brains.

After the satisfying meal, he sat quietly on the bank, the water swirling around his front paws. He burped loudly and licked the blood off his muzzle and wiped his face. He moved further up the slope and lay down on the bank, head between paws, and slept. After several hours, he sat up. Normally, flies did not bother him, but now he felt annoyed. A swarm had started following him everywhere. They crawled all over his face and chest, eating and laying eggs in the bits of dried blood and flesh. He crawled into the stream and lay down, nuzzling the bottom sand and gravel with his face. The cold water felt good. As he crawled forward in the stream, the gravel scrubbed most of the blood and gore away. He drank long then stood, shaking off the water and flies in a big spray, and started home.

Josiah called her the Judas cow. He explained, "Because she will lead the bear to slaughter instead of us, and we'll spare her if we can." Robert called her the bait cow. For two days, the bait cow did not attract the bear's attention. So, James McKay and Michael Tall Corn rode slowly up the trail, moving north along the eastern flank of the Sangre de Cristos. They paused often to listen and sniff the air. For all their scouting, they had not seen or heard from the bear since their arrival. If their purpose was to scout out the bear, learn about it, then kill it without getting killed, they were not doing very well. It seemed like the bear had left the country, and James secretly hoped that was the case. A few more days like

177

this and he would round up the boys and ride home. Story over. Thank the Almighty.

James pointed and whispered, "The vaqueros died down the hill there."

Michael studied the ground from his horse then dismounted. He noticed something. "I'm going to walk up the hill. Look around."

James nodded and dismounted.

They tied their horses loosely to the limb of a downed oak tree. If the horses persisted in a panic, they could get loose, perhaps escaping the bear. But a casual pull on the lead rope would not free them.

Michael could see what appeared to be a vague trail, the disturbed trees and brush of something passing— limbs twisted slightly or turned oddly, rocks slipped out of their old pockets. Anyone else might have missed some of these clues. Michael thought perhaps the trail was just a convenient route for occasional use. They moved up the hill where the trail stood out more distinctly. He knelt, studying sheared off trees, broken limbs and displaced rocks, and frowned. Several times in the past, the bear had charged down the hill along this distinct route, but Michael could scarce comprehend the damage. The creature had charged like a cannonball bent on striking and destroying the object of its wrath, and some trees had actually been sheared off. He had never seen anything like it.

James fingered the shattered tree trunk. "This is...scary."

Michael nodded. "Like a boulder cut loose."

"Maybe it was."

"Look here." He pulled some brown hairs from the bark and handed them to James, then carefully and quietly started up the hill. If the bear used this trail more than once, maybe a den was close by.

James moved to the left, always in sight. They were in no hurry. The wind came off their left shoulders, blowing mostly due north. In the back of his mind, James wondered what would happen if the wind changed direction and blew up the ridge, announcing their presence. The bear could be anywhere. And what would they do now, if they heard the bear coming? He glanced down the hill; the horses were too far away. His hand slipped down to his right revolver and absently brushed the walnut grip to flip off the trigger thong. He noticed what he had done and a grim smile crossed his face, briefly, a flicker of humor in a humorless situation. He remembered Gideon shouting for him to shoot the mountain lion, or him, as they fought, and he broke into a rare, real smile.

179

Michael squawked like a wounded crow, pointing up the hill to the right. James worked his way over to him. Neither spoke. He could see a granite rock outcropping and what might be a projecting shelf. Michael led off, easing more to the right. Slowly, carefully, they crept along.

When young, he and Michael got the notion one day to slap a bear. Some of the village women reported a large black bear down at the blackberry thicket. Michael's father, Chief Yellow Fox, forbid anyone to go down there until the bear had his fill and left the area. It started with boasting.

"I'm not afraid of any old bear," James had proclaimed, arms defiantly crossed on his chest.

This greatly irritated Michael, who thought he was the better of the two. "I am more brave," Michael retorted.

Back and forth they went, until James said, "I'll show you. I'll slap that old bear on the rump." Michael looked skeptical. They had both heard of bear slapping in the past, but not by anyone they knew. It was more of a myth or a legend.

To prove his point, James headed out at a jog and Michael followed. But when they drew near the thicket, Michael took the lead. Soon they heard the old boar, grunting blissfully, as he gobbled up the fat juicy blackberries. Michael led them through the aspen trees to a spot directly behind the bear, only forty feet.

James touched Michael's shoulder and crept by him. The wind was in his face. He moved quietly but steadily until within ten feet. He paused so long that Michael assumed he had lost his nerve. On a whim, Michael walked quickly toward James until they were standing side by side, just behind the busy bear.

James held up his right hand, three fingers showing. He threw his hand forward to show two fingers. He threw it forward again, showing one finger. After a brief pause, he leapt forward, Michael at his side. They both slapped the bear.

To their utter surprise, the seven-hundred-pound brute spun around as if on a swivel. They had thoroughly frightened the bear, who had never been attacked in its life, especially from behind. The large bruin's reaction was a predictable fear, quickly replaced by a vast rage. If he had lunged forward just then, he would have certainly caught one of the unfortunate youths. But out of habit and instinct, he raised up on his hind feet to better fight these dangerous assailants. Before he knew it, the two attackers were sprinting away, laughing hysterically. He gave chase, but the two easily wove between the aspen trees and slowly pulled away. After less than a two hundred feet, he pulled up, sniffing the air, his shock worn off. He licked his juice-covered lips and remembered the berries. The blackberry thicket called.

Unbeknownst to James and Michael, Michael's uncle, Spotted Owl, had seen the whole spectacle. The boys would not tell the story for fear of getting caught disobeying Michael's father. But around the fire that evening, Spotted Owl beckoned everyone to draw near, for he had a new story to tell, one of amazing adventure and daring. The whole tribe gathered around. Soon he had them spell bound as he related the tale of two fearless boys. He embellished the story greatly, adding heroic dialog and daring moves. As he neared the end, James and Michael knew he was talking about them and decided to sneak away, but Spotted Owl held Michael's arm.

At the end, he stood, pulling Michael and James up with him. "Here are the two heroes," he announced. "The two who courageously slapped the big bear, who fearlessly faced him when he turned, and laughed when he gave chase."

Even Michael's father had to smile, shaking his head at their audacity.

CHAPTER FOURTEEN

The late afternoon warm sun painted the forest tree tops in shades of yellow and light green. Birds flittered through the underbrush; a golden eagle screeched from high above the ridge, drifting on the warm air currents. Down the hill, gray tree squirrels argued over something, and occasional clouds cast the forest in temporary shadow. A perfect day by all accounts.

James looked over the edge of the shelf first then motioned Michael up on his right. They studied the cave entrance. The hair on the back of James's neck stood on end and his nostril's flared. An oily smell permeated the air, bringing to his senses a primitive anticipation of outright danger, like a physical thing. With difficulty, he slowed his breathing. James thought, how many hunters over the centuries had experienced just this feeling when hunting something that could actually kill them. This was not like hunting deer. Not even like slapping that old black bear. No, not at all. It was more like living with Mr. Cooper, during the last few months of the war; the dangerous mountain man had been hired by the Union army to assassinate the McKay Rangers.

What in the world were they doing? If the bear were actually in the cave, it could rush out and kill them—in a second. They were taking an unnecessary chance, something he had expressly forbidden the men to do. Between him and Michael, they carried two Henry rifles and four revolvers. Probably not enough firepower for what might lay before them.

Michael touched James's right elbow. With his hand, he pointed at James then the ground, then himself and the cave.

James shook his head and mouthed, "Together." Like always.

Michael nodded solemnly, right eyebrow arching skeptically.

They had been raised as brothers—James and Michael—among the Shawnee and the McKay plantation. Inseparable. As James grew older, he made allowances for his little brother, Henry, to spend more time with him. But Michael had been his first brother.

They crawled over the edge and crept soundlessly on moccasin feet up to the cave's right side. If the bear were inside and looked out, it would not see them. At the side of the cave, James leaned over, looking in. Nothing. He leaned farther. Nothing. Down the hill, the gray squirrels continued to argue, and he thought about hunting them for Ma's squirrel dumpling stew.

"I don't think he's home," James whispered softly.

Michael just looked at him. Was he sure? How would they know unless someone went in? The bear could be at the back of the cave, watching them. Part of him said it would be a wise move to go back to the camp and plan what to do next. In fact, they didn't know if this was the cave the bear used. He looked down at the Henry rifle in his hands. He slowly pushed the lever down, quietly chambering a round. He started to step around James, but James held up his left arm, blocking him.

"Together," he whispered. James knew that what they were about to do was probably the dumbest thing they had ever done—ever. What would they do if the bear was just sitting there looking at them?

Michael nodded. They were like brothers. Attack together. Die together. He did not think two Henry rifles would kill the grizzly, but maybe the firepower would be enough to help them escape. Maybe. Hopefully. If they ran fast enough, dodging through the trees.

James took a deep breath and stepped around the corner, exposing himself in the cave opening. A draft of cold air hit his face and for a brief second, he thought it was over.

Michael stepped up next to him, then purposefully walked forward into the darkness. James watched, at the ready, drifting to his left for a better view. Michael went to the back of the cave—almost thirty feet—then back to the front. "No bear," he said simply.

"But it smells like he lives here," James said, walking past Michael. Sunlight from the front of the cave cast diffused light into the darkness, but not quite enough. His eyes slowly adjusted. The cave seemed to be deeper but narrowed further back. In the back-left corner, a thin crack—about sixteen inches wide—extended into the darkness, floor to ceiling. They would need a torch to explore that. He turned back to the entrance and stiffened in shock, catching his breath.

Michael, facing him, watched James's reaction and froze, eyes large, a look of abject alarm on his face. Should he run out of the cave or toward James?

James waved furiously, beckoning Michael to come toward him. Michael glanced over his left shoulder. The big bear was just walking into view at the front of the cave. The beast was incredibly, impossibly large. He was looking straight across at the bear, and figured it was at least seven feet tall or more at the shoulders. The cave was barely big enough for him. Michael jumped toward James. James turned, crawling deeper into the cave, wriggling through the narrow crack.

Great Bear hesitated at the cave entrance, startled. He had seen something move, but was not quite sure. Were his eyes playing tricks again? Was it another bear? He had killed his tormentor, hadn't he? Then his nostrils flared automatically, as the scent of his favorite food drifted around and through his large muzzle. His eyes narrowed. A deep rumbling began in his chest. He stood. His roar shook the earth. Dust sprinkled down from the cave ceiling. He dropped to all fours, swiping at the ground with both front feet—left, right—then charged forward.

James squeezed sideways, scrambling deeper into the crack with Michael pushing from behind, but they soon ran out of room. The darkness deepened and James could not see. He reached above his head, grasping, feeling for something to lift them up and out of the narrow passage. He found a projection and pulled himself up, his legs spreading to stand on both sides of the narrow cave walls.

Michael grunted.

James looked down. The bear's arm reached deep into the opening, probing, clawing, trying to catch them.

Michael fired his Henry rifle; the explosion sounded incredibly loud in the confined space, causing their ears to ring. The bear roared and pulled back. Michael fired again. The bear reached in suddenly, and with a claw hooked the rifle's front sight, pulling it from Michael's grasp. He couldn't believe it and pulled out a revolver.

James found a narrow ledge and hauled himself up. He turned, reaching down. "Michael, give me your hand!"

Michael fired three times in quick succession. The bear roared louder. He looked up at James. "My bullets are only making him mad."

With renewed outrage and madness, the bear tore at the narrow opening, quickly and repeatedly swiping, tearing away rock and dirt. The cave filled with thick dust. None of the bullets hurt him, but the loud noise made his head hurt and his eyes blazed in renewed hatred. Like the mad beast he was, he chewed viciously at the opening, ripping rocks left and right, then he backed up and swiped repeatedly at the crack in the wall. The narrow opening began to widen, dirt and rocks flying. He reached deep inside, up to his shoulder and grabbed something. Like pulling the fresh, pliant meat from a walnut, he tried to pry out the prize. Almost got it, just a little more.

188

James grabbed Michael's outstretched hand, which was desperately waving and searching over his head in the dark. He managed to get both hands around Michael's right hand and wrist, pulling hard.

"Use your legs on the walls!" James yelled above the roaring bear.

Michael's legs were already three feet off the cave floor, feet pressed into the walls, the bear's searching claws just below. Michael lunged upward. They locked wrists with both hands. James began to pull him up, when suddenly, Michael was pulled back. James almost lost him, Michael's sweaty right hand slipping from is grasp.

James's Henry rifle slipped off the ledge, clattering to the cave floor. The bear pulled it immediately into the cave. As the bear swept the rifle by him, it flew out the front of the cave and over the ledge into the forest below.

"I've got you," James gasped, lifting Michael.

Michael used his legs to push off the narrow walls of the crack. James reached down and grabbed the back of his pants, pulling him the rest of the way onto the narrow ledge. Michael lay back, panting. The ledge was barely adequate; two grown people could not lay down, but they could sit.

In the near darkness, James felt along Michael's legs. As he suspected, warm blood. Down below them, the bear continued to roar and tear at the opening. Dust filled the narrow space, sending them into fits of coughing. James took off his shirt and tore it into strips and wrapped Michael's legs tightly. The right leg seemed worse. Michael's leg was bloody below the knee, but he thought he had the bleeding stopped.

Michael panted. "That was too close."

James put a hand on Michael's shoulder, shaking it gently. "I'm going to search back into the cave and see if we can get out that way." He squeezed his arm. "Michael?"

"Okay," Michael whispered hoarsely and coughed again.

"Don't move. The ledge is narrow."

"I know," Michael whispered. "Be careful."

James stood shakily and Michael lay down. James pushed off the opposite wall with his left hand, turned and reached over his head. His hand wrapped around a projecting rock, and he pulled himself up part way. The bear continued to roar and tear into the opening below, which was growing larger. He did not expect the bear to reach them, now that they were eight feet into the crack and eight feet up. But how determined was the beast?

Did it tire like normal animals, or was its great size matched by great strength and unlimited endurance?

Directly over his head, the ceiling seemed to widen. He found a foothold on the opposite wall across from the ledge they were on, pushing upward. Above his head, the rock was smooth and rounded, sloping away from him. He kept reaching, searching for something to grab onto. He jumped up a little—a dangerous move, because if he slid back, he might miss the narrow ledge below and fall to certain death below. At the limit of his reach, his middle finger on his right hand fell into a narrow crack. He hoped it was enough. His left leg pushed off the opposite side of the cave and he pulled himself up, his left hand searching for a purchase. He found another crack in the rock and pulled himself the rest of the way up the steep slope.

"There's more room up here," he announced. "I'll look around for a way out and be right back."

"I'll be here," Michael answered in the distance, then broke into a hacking cough.

James stood and abruptly bumped his head. He had lost his hat somewhere. He dropped to all fours, searching along the floor. The dark was so profound, he could not see his hand in front of his face. The cave was cool and seemed deep.

He crawled along on hands and knees, until his right hand suddenly dropped out from under him. He hit the floor with his chin. Okay, won't go that way, he thought. He moved left, deeper into the cave, reaching all around. His hand touched a wall on the left. He stood tentatively, searching for the cave wall and ceiling with a waving hand while tentatively sliding his feet along the floor. How long he traveled, he did not know. It felt like he was taking too long, but he reasoned that turning back without learning what might be ahead was not an option. Their only hope of escape might be this way. He crept along, carefully.

As he slowly shuffled forward, the smell of wet earth grew stronger. His left hand brushed something airy. Might be roots, he thought. He felt around over his head. When he pulled on the roots, dirt rained down. Something large scurried down his left arm. He shook it off and gathered the roots in his hands and pulled hard. Large chunks of dirt hit his head. He kept working in the darkness, a feeling of excitement rising. With the next pull of roots and dirt, a small beam of light filled the chamber. He felt instant relief and dug frantically, widening the opening. Finally, he pulled himself up, blinking at the brightness. The sun was just rising, shining through the forest. He realized he had been searching the back of the cave all night.

He continued to widen the hole, but a big tree root kept it from getting large enough to crawl through. He growled and started again in a spot three feet to the left. The ceiling was higher and more difficult to reach, but it was the best he could do. He worked feverishly, clawing and tearing at the roots and dirt. His frantic efforts reminded him of the bear, trying to get at them. Maybe he should roar in frustration and anger, he thought grimly. And he would start carrying a knife after today. He had to stop and gather the fallen dirt, so he could stand on the mound and reach higher. The dirt above his head was thicker than the other place, the work slow, but finally a new shaft of light broke through. He knew his fingers were bleeding, but he kept digging upward until the opening was wide enough for his shoulders. He piled more of the dirt onto the mound at his feet and jumped. He was able to hold on and slowly hoist himself up, but his revolvers stopped him—too wide. He dropped back down, took off the gun belt, threw it out, then hauled himself up and out.

He walked along the slope and looked around to orient himself. He moved north. The trees were thick in places. He finally spotted the top of the cave and looked back, estimating the distance. He thought he must have crawled through the cave for about a mile or more in total darkness. He sighed. And he had to go back in.

He could not hear the bear. The wind touched his right shoulder, so his scent would not—should not—carry toward the cave. He quietly walked around the area until he found what he wanted: several very dry sticks and dry moss. While keeping careful watch, he gathered as much dry moss as he could find then dropped back into the hole he had dug. He tied the moss to the sticks with strips of bark, then used the end of his revolver to strike the flint he always carried to start a fire in the moss. He would use one torch to go back to Michael and the other to get back out. Hopefully.

As he worked his way through the cave, he came upon the place where his hand dropped out from under him. He paused at the edge of a deep, ominous opening. With his toe, he nosed a two-inch rock over the edge. He waited but did not hear it hit bottom. Then something else caught his attention. On the wall opposite, flickering in the torch light not ten feet way, blazed a vein of gold and quartz all of forty inches wide, running down the wall from the ceiling into the darkness of the pit.

"We're rich," he muttered without feeling.

He continued to a fork in the cave and knelt on the floor to determine which direction he had crawled during the night—the right passage. The ceiling dropped to five feet. After thirty feet the ceiling rose and the floor widened. He walked quicker, but then the ceiling dropped to about four feet. He crawled into what seemed like a small room. On the far side he noticed the hint of light from the cleft in the back of the cave; the place where he began.

He leaned out, carefully looking over the rounded edge. Morning light from the cave entrance cast a pale glow through the narrow opening.

"Michael," he called softly. No answer. Maybe he's sleeping. He leaned out further. "Michael," he called with a little more urgency. He leaned out as far as he safely could without falling, just able to see half of the ledge below. Michael was gone. Fear welled up inside him. "Michael!" he whispered loudly. Oh, Michael, he thought with despair. His heart sank in his chest and his eyes watered.

He had never planned to climb back down there. He had expected Michael to reach up, so he could pull him to the next level. Could he get back down without sliding off the round rock? He lay down on his stomach and put his feet out over the drop. As he inched back, he found the cracks he had put his fingers in. If he missed getting his fingers into the narrow slots, he could slide out over the edge, falling all the way to the bottom. Bear bait.

The left finger found the mark, but the right missed. He swung left, hanging precariously over the drop. His breath caught in his chest. He eased his finger out of the crack and soundlessly slid down until his left toes touched the narrow ledge, his right foot barely propped against the far wall.

He looked around in the dim light from the cave. He was surprised to see how much of the opening the bear had torn away. A normal-sized grizzly could have squeezed into the crack. He waited, listening. Nothing. Would he hear the bear, if it was sleeping? Very slowly and carefully, he lowered himself to the cave floor. In slow motion, he crept toward the opening until he could just glance around the corner into the cave.

The bear was not there. He let out the breath he did not know he had been holding. In the middle of the floor he spotted Michael's mangled, bloody moccasin. He reached down and picked it up tenderly. Michael must have rolled off the ledge during the night, he thought with an anguished heart. I should have taken him with me. He choked back a sob, instead sighing deeply and slowly. A single tear slipped down his dirty face, leaving a thin track. Michael had been his best friend all his life. They had grown up together; brothers in every way except mother. He carefully worked his way to the cave entrance. He glanced around the left corner. Nothing. He looked right. Nothing. Which way did the bear go? He did not want to attract attention or run into the bear, which might be nearby.

The horses. He would carefully crawl down the slope to the horses, if they were still there, and get away. He turned right, out of the cave, deftly working his way down the slope. When he cleared the thickest of the trees, the horses were standing two hundred feet away where they left them, and across the back of his horse, lay Michael. He jogged and slid down the rest of the way, not worried about the extra noise.

Michael was asleep.

James shook him gently. Michael roused, grinned at him, and closed his eyes.

"Okay. Let's get you back."

James swung into the saddle behind Michael, and took the reins to lead his own horse down the mountain to the herd.

CHAPTER FIFTEEN

Rhodes spotted the horses trotting in from the north. He started to smile then realized two people were riding on one horse. He pulled out the bull's horn and blew three sharp blasts to alert the search parties.

James and Michael rode into the camp five minutes later.

The first search party back was Robert, O'Keefe and Jefferson.

James sat by the fire, sipping coffee.

Robert said, "Sent a search party out this mornin', but they went more north of where you say the cave is."

Juan Ortega stepped back from the cot, drying his hands on a towel. "Best I can do. Bleed a lot. Clean good. Iodine. Twenty stitches right leg is all. Three shots bourbon." He smiled at that. Soon they would need more iodine *and* bourbon.

James walked over and rested his hand on Juan's shoulder. "Thank you. Michael is tough. He'll get through this." He thought Michael would recover, but probably limp for a month or two. The bear had cut his right leg with the huge claws, but not too deep. They would have to watch for infection.

"Your shirt keep from bleeding to death," Juan added.

Michael moaned and raised his arms, swinging them left and right, as if fighting off something.

"Fever," Juan said quietly. "Him fight bear."

James put his hand on Michael's sweaty forehead. The arms slowly lowered.

"He'll probably fight that bear the rest of his life," Robert said.

"Like you at Shiloh?" O'Keefe said, walking up. On some nights Robert woke up, yelling orders.

Robert looked at him angrily, frowning deeply. "Yeah, like me at Shiloh…and Sharpsburg, and Chancellorsville, and Wilderness…" As suddenly as it started, the anger fell away and he sighed, looking wistfully toward the hills. He turned and walked off.

James and Henry watched him jump on his horse and ride toward the herd. They could tell O'Keefe felt bad about bringing up the war, it still being so fresh in everyone's mind.

"Sorry about that boys," he mumbled and followed Robert, everyone assumed to apologize.

Henry sat down next to Michael's cot. "Robert saw more fighting than anyone and came away mostly unscathed, except for his battered soul "

Like us, James thought, keeping his feelings close. He would go along with nary a thought to the recent war and their many battles, then something would just jump up and bite him, reminding him of what all they had gone through. Like the gun battle with the rustlers. He knew the pent-up anger, sadness, and guilt suddenly erupted on the surface, like that old geyser the mountain men talk about up in the Wyoming Territory. Predictable, they said, down to the hour. He knew the recent Indian fight brought some of it to the surface. After they settled down that evening after the fight, he remembered shooting the Indian who wanted to surrender. A nagging guilt sauntered around the back of his mind, swatting at his conscience like an annoying fly. He wanted to squash the thing and be at peace. But deep in his heart, he knew it was wrong, killing an enemy that wanted to surrender.

The worrisome part though was that another part of his mind didn't care. Still another part, maybe the most hidden chamber of his mind, seldom visited, enjoyed the act of revenge, the taste of battle, and the secretive joy of killing the deserving enemy. He knew his act was a type of murder. He wouldn't want to argue the fine points of combat, or the passion of killing in the heat of battle. When the Indian raised his hands, essentially giving up, the nature of the battlefield had changed. Further killing became murder, a sin, a black stamp on his soul. In a court he could quibble about the merits of the brief battle, or the suffering of his men and his heart; could probably even parlay an acquittal—his enemy being an Indian and all, but he knew it was wrong—plain and simple. Type of murder? No, not really. It was just murder. He was a murderer. He shook his head at the mental admission, not that he would share his thoughts with anyone. A confession never spoken aloud, but shame, nonetheless.

He knew his wife, Margaret, whom everyone called Peggy, was a leveling force in his life. She kept him steady. When, at times, the war intruded on his thoughts and soul and mood, Peg had a way of lightening his attitude without trying. She had a way of somehow knowing what he was feeling, going through, and needed. A soft touch. A soft word. Closeness. Stillness. Warmth and caring. A laugh that warmed his heart and beckoned for more. He just enjoyed spending time with her. They were best friends.

After washing the cave dirt off, he made a fresh pot of coffee, poured a cup, and rode his horse out onto the prairie to be alone with his thoughts. If anything happened to her, his world would simply come to an end.

The next morning, Michael hitched himself up on his left elbow. James sat on the edge of the cot. At first, Michael acted like he didn't know him, his forehead wrinkled in concentration. Then his face showed recognition and the dawn of understanding.

"Feeling better?" James asked.

Henry and Josiah came over and squatted by the cot, set up beside the wagon.

Michael studied them for a minute then looked at his bandaged legs, nodding. "I remember now. You were gone." He reached up and rubbed the bruise on his head. "I fell off the ledge. Landed on the ground and lay there. Thought the bear would eat me for sure. But it didn't. I pulled myself up and looked into the cave. The bear was sleeping. Snoring. I just…" He shook his head to clear the momentary confusion. "I just walked out the front, picked up my Henry rifle and your rifle, and found your hat, and went for my horse." He looked at James. "The next thing I knew, you were shaking me awake."

"I found another way out and went back for you." James paused, choking back his raw emotion, a mixture of guilt and fear. "I thought…I thought the bear…ate you…because your moccasin was in the middle of the cave floor."

"I'm very glad you both came back safe," Henry said. He knew two things: They had done something incredibly stupid, and they had somehow gotten incredibly lucky.

"Was close," James whispered. "Too close."

"Josiah had us praying non-stop for you all to come back safe and sound," Henry said.

"Truth be told, we were worried sick," Josiah added. "Someone was praying 'round the clock."

Michael took Josiah's hand, shaking it lightly. "We made it. We are alive. That's enough."

"That's enough," Josiah said with feeling. "Thank God."

"Yes, thank God," Michael repeated.

Juan Ortega walked up, carrying a bucket of water for the stew. "Need to get ready for rain."

Henry looked at the sky. Long white horsetail clouds stretched from west to east. "Today?"

"Feel it—in my old bones," he said, shrugging. "Tonight, I think." He felt something else, but how to describe it? A heaviness, like suffocating, foreboding. Maybe it was just the weather. He looked anxiously at the sky.

"Rain. And now we know the bear is actually here," James said.

"When you went into the cave, were you thinking it would be empty, because the bear wasn't around here anymore?" Gideon asked.

James looked at Gideon then Michael and back to him, thinking. "That's it, surely. After so long without any hint of his presence, I thought he had moved on. I really did. We would not find him in his lair, and then we would head home today. The cave was empty. And we didn't even know if that was the right cave. Maybe it isn't even now, and he just came by. Don't know." He looked at the clouds. "I've got to be sure we are ready." The one scenario he feared most was about to happen: rain, utter darkness, and a potential bear attack.

CHAPTER SIXTEEN

G reat Bear awoke and sat up. After a few minutes, he walked groggily out of the cave and over the ridge to the river on the western side of the mountains. He drank heavily then lay on the bank in the sunshine. He could not remember anything about the strangers in his cave. Late in the afternoon, he crossed the river, moving west, following honeybees to a hive high up in a dead tree and ate most of the honey. The persistent and deep headache left him feeling exhausted. He crawled into a clump of weather-downed trees and slept uneasily.

Hailstones slamming into his face woke him. On any day, he walked around half angry all the time, and these sky stones hurt. Now he flew into a flaming rage with nothing to lash out at. He stood, swaying, and raised his face to the sky, bellowing and snarling. The clouds seemed to answer with a long roll of thunder. He swiped at the sky with both paws. Lightning struck the side of the mountain, splitting a tall pine. He roared and attacked, charging across the river and up the hill. When he reached the broken tree, a feeble trail of smoke rose from the shattered, twisted trunk, raindrops sizzling on the coals. He swiped angrily at the tree, tearing off big chunks of bark. He bit viciously. Then, his energy spent, he sat studying the burning coals. The hail stopped, but the heavy rain continued. His stomach rumbled.

With a heave, he stood and walked up the hill and over the ridge to his cave. As he started to enter, a scent drifted through the heavy rain. His eyes narrowed and he turned to investigate.

Juan was right. Just before sunset, a ferocious hailstorm announced the coming rain. There was not enough room under the wagon for everyone, but they crammed together as best they could, using the tarp and extra saddle blankets to shield the worst of the storm.

"That hail is the size of a small apple," Henry noted.

They had pulled most of the horses in close and saddled those they could to protect their backs. Still, the poor horses shifted and turned as the beating continued. The strong wind began to blow the rain sideways. Off in the distance another rolling rumble of thunder met their ears.

"Coming closer," Gideon noted.

Through the heavy rain, they watched the cattle run off in the dark. "Cattle have stampeded," Robert said quietly to no one in particular.

"How long you figure this poundin' will continue?" Wizzy asked. He was in the middle of the group to keep any possibility of rain off his head.

James leaned to the left, looking up. A flash of lightning flitted between clouds high above. "Maybe an hour or so, until that big flat top thunderhead passes by."

"How can you tell it's a flat top?" Wizzy asked.

"Saw it coming for us at supper time."

"Oh. I was chasing that no-account calf again, the one that's always wandering off."

Henry huffed. "That *calf* must weigh five hundred pounds, if he weighs an ounce."

"Now old Gustaf, bless his soul, could read the weather, that one could," O'Keefe started. "Said a sailor's life might depend on how they interpreted the weather and then positioned the ship."

"How's that?" Marcus asked.

"Well, should they suspect serious weather bearin' down on'm, the ship might hightail it to a safe harbor to ride out the storm."

Marcus laughed. "Like when we ran home from town just before the big snow hit."

"Much the same, laddie, much the same."

"We're at the mercy of the weather most times," Robert said philosophically. "Was camped out in the Big Bend country, east of the Santiago Mountains one time — west Texas. We set up in a wash to get outta the wind, which was blowin' hard and almighty bitter cold. A light rain with a touch of snow at sundown and all. So, the four of us, Pa, cousin Jack, Wilber and me, we was sleepin' like a flock of contented sheep, when the wagon gives a jolt. Was dark 'nough to cut with a dull knife. So, I just naturally jumped outta the back of the wagon. Next thing you know, I'm swimmin'!"

"Swimming?" Wizzy said.

"Well, nears we could figure, it was barely rainin' down in the valley, whilst up on the mountain ten or twenty miles away, it was rainin' somethin' powerful. Maybe a rain and snow mix. Whilst we slept, the water come down the arroyo and floated our wagon like a boat. We traveled near two miles like that afore she settled down, me holdin' onto the wagon seat the whole time."

"Were you scared?" Marcus asked. He was scared just listening to the story.

"Mostly. There was no light, not at all. No stars. No moon. Purely black, and then there we were in a river of water, and us flailin' around like a bunch of drownin' cats. Went down two, three times, afore I got my bearin's and grabbed onto that seat. Actually, Pa said we was lucky the wagon floated or we coulda all drowned. Probably. As it was, we lost half our provisions. Horses musta heard it comin', 'cause they got outta that arroyo afore the water hit."

"Tough way to learn a lesson," Henry noted.

James chuckled lightly. "Sometimes you have to pass the test before you realize Mother Nature has you in school."

"I think that's one reason why we tell stories," O'Keefe said. "As a way of teachin' people about our mistakes, so's they don't repeat'm."

Wizzy understood. "So, no matter how cold the wind is or how rainy, settin' up camp in a dry steam bed is always a poor idea."

"That's right," Robert said, patting his shoulder.

Henry said, "You know, why don't we tell stories like that in the evening—stories about survival and learning, so others can gain a lesson or two from them?" They already talked around the evening fire, but not purposefully trying to teach a lesson that might help others.

"Would have to be true stories," James added, looking at O'Keefe through the lantern light, his right eyebrow raised. "Not embellished to make them better or worse—just the facts of the matter."

The men murmured agreement. They all had similar stories, where they could have died or been severely injured, but had somehow, miraculously escaped, especially those that had survived the recent war. Or, in having passed through the tribulation, a person came out the other side with a tale so amazing, some would scarce believe it."

"Like that Hugh Glass," James said. "The mama grizzly tore him to pieces. Even parts of his ribs were exposed on his back. His friends left him to die and he crawled for two hundred miles to the fort."

"Crawled? Two hundred miles?" O'Keefe said. "That's incredible." He didn't believe it.

"Was in 1823," James said. "He was fur trapping and exploring with General Ashley up on the Missouri River. After the bear got him, the others lit out, thinking him dead. So, he had to crawl to Fort Kiowa."

There was more to the story, but James held his hand out in the rain. "Letting up some."

Robert stretched and unfolded his long legs, and stood. "Might be lettin' up some, but we'll get soaked either way gatherin' the cattle. So, let's git to it. Come a mornin', they'll be in New Mexico or back in Denver, if we don't start now." He climbed onto his roan and disappeared into the dark.

"You heard him," James said, climbing onto his black stallion, and he was gone.

No one moved for a slow count of ten. Then, one by one, they left the relative warmth and dry of the close bodies and blankets under the wagon. Marcus quickly gathered the four horses of the remuda that had pulled away from the ropes—they hadn't wandered far, and staked them downwind of the wagon with the others.

Despite the steady rain, Juan and Whipple started a fire. They kept dry wood and buffalo chips in a tarp. Whipple stood over the sputtering fire with his coat open to protect the fragile flame from the rain until it got going. Because the smoke swirled about him, he smelled like burning cow turds.

Juan Ortega turned and gave a start, dropping the half-filled coffee pot. He thought Whipple was the Angel of Death. With his arms outspread, and the long, black coat hanging down, framed by the growing firelight, Juan knew his time had finally come. He made the sign

213

of the cross three times, muttering *Hail Marys*, until he regained his composure.

He put the large coffee pot on the fire and glared up at the young man. "Whipple! Go cut up bacon for breakfast," he said irritably.

Great Bear slowly walked down the side of the mountain, stopping occasionally to sniff the air. The rain began to let up. There! He caught the scent again, flitting up from somewhere below. He continued down the mountain and turned north. After two miles, a canyon mouth opened up on his left.

If the cattle were a little smarter, they would have charged past the bear to the freedom of the prairie beyond. But they sniffed the approaching brute and ran into the box canyon, eyes rolling up in crazed fear, not realizing they were trapped. When they came to the end, all they could do was turn, and wait. Some moaned. No-Account calf looked up the steep slope. Instinct alone told him to at least try to escape.

He scrambled over the loose rocks and debris, often falling to his face and knees; then, for lack of purchase, even climbed using his knobby knees. He bawled like the calf he still was and scrambled upward. Soon his knees were badly scraped and bleeding. Down below, he heard the bear attack.

The other young calf went down, viciously torn to pieces. The bear began eating the calf, while the two cows watched with wild eyes. Suddenly, No-Account's mother leapt forward, charging past the bear. The bear realized too late what she was up to. Although his right paw swept outward, he only scraped her hind leg as she bravely scooted by.

The other cow was another matter. When the first cow ran forward, she hesitated a few seconds and then followed. But now Great Bear realized what was going on. As the cow tried to escape past him, he lunged forward, tackling the cow while tearing open her throat. He stood, roaring in victory. Then went back to eating the warm calf.

No-Account calf scrambled up the steep slope to the top and over the ridge. He turned left, following a vague trail southward. When another well-used trail crossed in front of him, by some primitive instinct he knew to turn left again and started down the long slope heading east. An hour after his mother found the herd, he limped in, terrified and exhausted.

The sky was growing light through the black clouds and steady rain. The exhausted, wet weary men gathered around the wagon for breakfast. Juan prepared bacon, beans, and dried apples.

"Did you hear that roar?" Thomas Rhodes asked. "Up north of here."

Emilio nodded. "I hear." The looked at each other, not trying to mask their fear.

"By my count, we're still missing eight," James said.

"Yeah, and did you see Wizzy's calf?" Robert asked. "Knees're all tore up, and his mama has five scrapes along her right hind leg, like what a big griz might make whilst tryin' to get ahold a her."

"You think the grizzly got the others?" Wizzy asked, eyes large.

"Likely," James said. "Some ran south, but others ran north." He looked around. "Where's Henry and Josiah?"

Thomas rode up and jumped down. "Henry's coming in with six."

Through flashes of lightning in the clouds above, Henry and Josiah followed some of the cattle northward, the fresh tracks muddy and filling with water They found six huddled under a few lone pine trees.

"Want to flip to see who takes these six back?" Henry asked.

"Why don't we take them back together?" Josiah asked.

"Because I figure from the tracks, there's at least four more ahead."

"You take them back. I'll look around until morning, then head back."

"You sure?" Henry asked.

"Yeah, go. Come on back out and help, if I'm not back by breakfast."

They started the cattle south, then Josiah turned back north. When the clouds lit up with lightning, he could see hoof prints in the soft prairie, filling with fresh rain water. "Yep, heading north," he murmured.

He lost the prints several times but eventually started up the canyon. He wished the lightning would flash again to make sure. He had the makings for a fire, but doubted he could put together anything in this weather. Should have brought one of the lanterns, he thought. If nothing else, he would wait under a tree out of the rain until daylight. The cattle were probably under some trees up ahead drier than him.

The longhorn cow charged out of the brush and barreled into his horse, knocking him over. Josiah hit the ground hard, the wind knocked out of him. As he stood, he realized the mud had broken his fall, or he might have broken a rib or two. His horse shot down the canyon, following the cow. Lighting flashed through the clouds above and he sighed sadly. He hated being afoot. The boys would rile him about going for a stroll in the morning rain, or some such teasing. He smiled to think of it. Nothing to do but follow his horse or head to the camp.

The bear roared.

Josiah's eyes bulged in fear. The bear was close. Too close. Where to go? If the bear smelled him, it would run him down. He desperately looked all around. Running after his horse now was out of the question; it was too dark to see. He needed to get into a tree or high on some rocks. He started up the steep canyon slope. At first, the going was easy then it became steeper. He didn't mind. The steeper the better. Finally, he was reaching up, like climbing a ladder, pulling himself from bush to bush and rock to rock. In the lightning, he spotted an old lightning struck tree off to his right and worked his way over to it. He slipped on some rocks and slid down the steep slope for over fifty feet. He was bruised and cut. Should have gone with Henry, he thought wistfully. He heard the approach of huffing and ominous scratching sounds below him.

Josiah's heart pounded in his chest. He did not want to die to this bear. He did not want to be eaten by any animal. He choked back a sob and scrambled upward, knuckles and fingers bloody, knees torn. Chin bloody from slipping forward onto his face. He prayed for lightning, because he could not see the black tree in the darkness. The lightning flashed. There! The tree was right in front of him.

At one time, the ancient pine had stood over one hundred feet tall. Now the old pine was broken in two, the base sixty feet tall with the top forty feet lying beside it. The ancient tree had watched over this canyon and the prairie beyond for almost two hundred years, before lightning cut it down, the top portion sheared off by the violent strike over twenty years before. The base of the old pine appeared to have an opening, a darker section. Without a second thought to what might be in there, Josiah crawled into the space and started climbing.

In less than a minute, the wide tree shook and the bear roared. Josiah moaned. He could hear a raccoon family chittering above him. He accidently slipped back but caught his left boot heal on a knobby interior projection.

Down below the bear growled continuously while swiping and biting at the opening. Josiah climbed up twenty feet and stopped. It was getting tight. He thought, I should be safe here. How long until Henry returns? Then he hoped Henry came with help and not alone. If Henry comes back alone, he'll be killed outright.

CHAPTER SEVENTEEN

After Great Bear killed the second cow, he roared in victory and went back to eating the calf. With his great claws, he opened up the calf and feasted. His muzzle and long tongue searched the chest cavity, devouring the visceral organs. He lifted his muzzle, sniffing the air all around him, the wind blowing up the narrow canyon. Even in the rain, he knew that smell. Humans! He stood, turning his head left and right, then he turned around, facing down the canyon toward the prairie, the east wind in his face. Yes! He galloped, a happy feeling flooding his body. The calf was good. But humans!

He ran too far and stopped to sniff. He turned, grunting irritably and walked back up the canyon, muzzle methodically swinging back and forth. Up the hill? He turned to the right. With his long, black, arched claws, he pulled his great mass up the steep slope. The smell grew stronger, relentlessly urging him on. Spots of blood on the sharp rocks inflamed his passion and bloody drool began falling from his heavy jaws. At the old tree the human smell overwhelmed his mind. He felt delirious with joy. He roared. His prize was right here, hiding in the tree. The old burnt bark broke away easily. His great jaws ripped away large segments. Although five feet wide, the ancient, decayed tree shuddered and began to lean. Somewhere up inside the tree, the human creature screamed in terror.

Josiah wept.

"Dear God in heaven, don't let me die like this!" he shouted into the darkness. "Please Lord, have mercy on me!" He recited the Lord's Prayer, more crying the words than saying them.

As the tree began to lean, he knew his life was on the verge of ending horribly. He screamed and fired his pistol down past his feet, but in the total darkness, he had no idea whether he hit anything or not. Six shots. The bear continued to tear at the tree. He pulled his other pistol and pointed it between his legs. The bear grunted below him. He fired—nothing. "What!" he cried. He pulled back the trigger and fired again—nothing. The powder must be wet. Although his long coat usually kept his revolvers dry, the left one must have gotten wet when his horse went down. He tried the remaining four cylinders—nothing. He moaned. He did not have the fixings to reload, not to mention trying to do it up in the dark tree.

I have to get home to my wife and kids, he thought. And he had a church full of people who depended on him. "Dear Lord, deliver me from evil!" he cried. "Dear Lord, are you listening?" The tree leaned more. The bear continued a constant grunting and growling, while viciously tearing and biting at the tree base. If he survived this, he might not sleep for a year, thinking about this night. How could he survive this persistent demon bear? Who ever heard of such a thing? My God, are you listening?

With a loud crack the tree shook and began a slow-motion plunge. Josiah tried to brace his body tighter. His only hope now was to ride it out, somehow. Dealing with the bear would come later, inevitably.

The old tree hit the slope hard and began to roll. Small saplings bent submissively at its passing. Small boulders broke loose and joined the fray. In short order, a landslide developed. Rocks, boulders and dead trees that had been perched precariously for centuries let loose and joined the big tree in its headlong tumble.

Great Bear followed at a walk, grunting happily, and licking his lips in anticipation.

After the first dozen revolutions, Josiah was knocked unconscious and flopped around inside like a rag doll. The tree gained speed. When it rebounded off a large boulder, it broke in half, and flew through the air for over a hundred feet, spinning wildly, the limp body ejected out the end. Josiah landed on the slope and unknowingly rolled into a crack in the rock face.

The old tree continued its reckless plunge into the valley below, pieces breaking off, and finally rolled to a stop near the canyon entrance. Great Bear walked up to the fallen tree and began sniffing and pawing at the broken trunk. He scooped out a fat raccoon that bit him on the paw. He growled annoyingly and bit off its head. Three other raccoons scurried by. He didn't care. He wanted his reward. The smell was strong. When Josiah was knocked unconscious, he had messed himself, and Great Bear loved the strong smell and tore into the tree, shredding the bark into little pieces.

Through the heavy clouds above, the sky began to lighten. Great Bear lay down, studying the inside of the tree. Only twenty feet remained of the sixty, and he could see through the center and out the other end. The human had escaped. How? Where? Great Bear grunted irritably and stood, shaking his coat free of water. He looked around, carefully inspecting the local area and nosing the wet ground. Nothing. The creature must have run away after the log stopped moving. It never occurred to him that his prey might still be up the slope.

After a few minutes, he walked out of the canyon and turned north. He did not know where he was going or why. He just felt like walking. The rain grew stronger.

Henry walked his horse up to the chuck wagon and climbed down. He was wet, tired, and sore. Whipple handed him a cup of hot coffee, and he savored the smell before taking a sip. Juan's lantern lit up the immediate area. The morning sky was beginning to lighten.

Out of habit, he did a quick headcount of the gathered men, nodding to James. "Brought back six from about four miles or so north of here."

"Then we are only missing two cows." James looked at Robert. "Not bad."

"Not bad, considering," Robert agreed, scanning the sky.

"Where's Josiah?" James asked.

Henry had started to walk away and turned back. "We were on the trail of four more. From your count, probably two more then. Anyhow, he's looking for them."

James frowned. Something troubled him. The idea of a lone rider out there with the bear on the loose just

225

bothered him at a basic level. He glanced at Gideon. Gideon nodded, right eyebrow arching. Without another word, they both walked to their horses.

"Hold on there," Henry called. "I'll go with you." He knew where they were going, and tossed the empty cup to Whipple.

The rain increased, mixed with tiny hailstones.

"That's where we found the six cattle," Henry said, pointing to the pine trees. The rain pounded them. Although late morning, the sky suddenly grew darker.

"Looky there," Gideon said, pointing. "Josiah's horse."

Behind the trees, Josiah's horse grazed on the short green grass.

"That's not good," James said quietly. He trotted up to the horse and took the reins. He did not notice blood anywhere on the rig, but the rain might have washed any off. "Damn," he said under his breath. The Henry rifle was still in the scabbard. As the horse turned, he noticed that the left side of the horse and saddle were caked in mud.

Gideon said, "I think the horse fell down, see that mud there. Probably ran off, leaving Josiah stranded."

"Oh no," Henry moaned.

"Dear Lord, I hope it wasn't the bear," Gideon said.

James' face grew hard; his mouth grim. He pulled out Josiah's Henry and chambered a round. The others did the same. He would empty Josiah's rifle into that wretched bear, then retrieve his own Henry and continue until the bear had more lead in it than teeth. And between them they had six revolvers. The time for patty-footing around these mountains was over. What they needed was direct violent action, and he was the man for it.

They walked their horses slowly, studying the ground and the terrain around them.

"He went up this canyon," Gideon said, pointing.

They spread out. A few hundred feet in, they found the lightning struck tree, where it had rolled to a stop.

"Henry, Gideon, stay in the saddle," James said. "Stay alert."

James climbed down and walked the length of the tree. "Dead raccoon over there—no head." Other pieces of the old pine lay off to the right. From all the pieces, he could tell it had once been over a hundred feet tall, and now only a small portion remained. At the base, he examined the chew and claw marks, shaking his head in disbelief. Reminded him of the cave. He felt along the ragged edges, then squat down to look inside. No Josiah.

He held his breath, wondering if the bear had pulled him out.

He stood, looking all around. He felt like crying. "I think Josiah was in this hollow tree. The bear tried to get him out, but there's no sign of him." He just could not imagine Josiah gone. He looked up the slope, examining the debris field. Where are you, Josiah, he wondered. He nodded, "Looks like the tree started up there and rolled down here."

Henry jumped off his horse and started up the slope.

James looked at Gideon. "Keep watch. We won't be long." James took out his Henry and handed Josiah's rifle to Gideon. "Remember, Gideon, this bear can outrun your horse."

Gideon frowned. He wished there was less brush in the canyon. The bear could be on him before he knew it was attacking in this lousy weather. "I'll be careful. You might see better from up there, anyway. Give a whistle, if you've a mind to."

James and Henry climbed the steep canyon to where the tree had stood.

"The tree was here," Henry said, sitting on the slope, hitching his collar up to keep the cold rain out, although he was already soaked from the neck down. "The bear pushed it over." He stood, studying the area. "And it must have rolled to the bottom. Do you think Josiah climbed up here?"

"I do. I think he got inside the tree," James said quietly. "Let's just follow the path." He thought they would find where the bear pulled Josiah out of the tree, or at least enough of their friend to bury.

They scurried and slipped sideways down the steep slope until they reached the big boulder.

James ran his hand over the rock, where the tree left a long scrapping mark. "The tree hit the boulder hard," he said. "See all of this bark. The scratch mark here."

Henry walked below the boulder and up the other side. "Turned it some. See how it headed more left for the canyon entrance."

James climbed across the face of the slope, slipping and sliding, more east and away from where they had originally climbed up the slope. The longer they looked for Josiah, the longer James could deny that the bear pried him out of the tree and dragged him off to be eaten. Surely there would have been more blood. He felt the deep despair of sudden loss, his heart aching. He had known Josiah all his life, but they had grown especially close in the last year of the war. He sat on an old gray log and studied the canyon from one end to the other. No sign of the bear.

Henry sat down next to him, his lower lip trembling. "Rotten way to go," he murmured, barely able to talk. "What will we tell Sarah?"

James sighed. "Can't rightly tell his wife a bear ate him." A curtain of heavy rain passed down the canyon until they could barely see Gideon below.

"Even if the bear ate him, we have to find what we can, wherever that takes us." Henry stood. "You know, for a burial." He could not imagine that the bear ate every last piece of their friend, clothes and all.

James stood also. "Look, Gideon is scouting down at the mouth of the canyon."

The rain began to let up. "What's that smell?" Henry asked.

"I smell it too," James said.

They slid down the canyon side but at more of an angle to the east.

"Lord Almighty!" Henry shouted.

The toe of Josiah's right boot stuck out of the crack a few inches. They would never have seen the boot unless standing right next to it.

James slid to a stop and looked in. "I think he's alive!"

"Thank the Good Lord!" Henry shouted. "Want me to pull his foot?"

"Hold on. He's breathing. Josiah!" James called. "Wake up, Josiah!"

They cleared loose rocks away that might fall down on him.

"How are we going to get him out of there?" Henry asked, hand on the boot toe.

"Look there. His left arm is broken," James said. The arm lay across his chest but at an odd angle. "Maybe we should pull his legs first and sort of drag him out."

James reached down and tried to grab a shoulder. "He's really jammed in there." He sat back, looking around. "He must have flown out of the tree when it struck that boulder. The bear missed him, somehow." He sighed. "Fortunately."

Henry wiped at his eyes. "Yeah, fortunately."

"I think we'll have to grab the leg sticking up there and the broken arm. Sort of lift him out sideways."

"Good thing he's unconscious," Henry murmured, grabbing the boot with both hands.

Henry gently pulled on the leg, trying to lift Josiah. James leaned over the crack, reaching down. The arm appeared to be broken between the elbow and wrist, so he grabbed the arm just above the elbow and pulled. Josiah didn't respond, so he pulled harder. The position was awkward. He couldn't quite get both hands down there—too deep. They needed help.

James leaned back. "We need Gideon and a rope."

Henry didn't say a word. He turned and started down the slope, half sliding, half running. He whistled loudly. Gideon heard the whistle and raced back, rifle at the ready.

"We found Josiah! But we need your help—need a rope and a blanket."

Gideon fairly ran up the slope.

As the three of them stood around Josiah, James studied the problem. "Okay, I'll get the arm again. Gideon reach in and get his belt. Henry lift the leg."

As they lifted Josiah's limp body out of the crack, he moaned. His eyes opened briefly. He looked around, a wild-eyed look on his face, then passed out.

They wrapped the blanket around him, tightly tied with ropes. It took almost an hour to ease Josiah down the slope. At the bottom they set him on Henry's horse, and Henry rode behind, holding him. The rain increased briefly then turned to a thin, wet snow. Although unconscious, Josiah began to shake.

"We need to hurry," Henry shouted over the rain. He spurred his horse into a smooth trot.

CHAPTER EIGHTEEN

Ortega made room for Josiah in the chuck wagon and started a fire in one of his big pots to warm the area. He set the arm first.

Henry sat with Josiah while Ortega worked on him. "He's hurt bad," Henry said quietly.

Ortega looked up at him. "Hit head hard." He actually thought Josiah hit his head too hard, but said nothing. He had seen men die from lesser wounds. With the arm set, they cleaned him up and Ortega felt around. "Four broke ribs, down low here. Leg should have break, but no. Bad bruised."

"Hang in there, Josiah," Henry whispered into his left ear. "We're praying for you." During the last year of the Civil War, Henry and Josiah were a sharpshooter team. Although Josiah spotted for Henry, he had a new Enfield rifle from the Asheville, North Carolina armory and could easily shoot small pinecones off a fence railing at two hundred yards—every twelve seconds—on a still morning.

The cowherders huddled around the sizzling fire. The snowflakes were small, but the sky turned white as the storm grew in intensity.

"Snowin' kinda late in the season," Robert noted with annoyance.

"Well, it's early June in Colorado," James said. "Probably not so unusual for up here. Look, it's too warm to stick anyhow."

O'Keefe laughed shortly. "Some gold camps in the Sierra Nevada mountains are only free of snow from mid-June to mid-September. You get your gold out or you spent the rest of the time hunkered down by the fire, probably starvin'."

Around noon, Josiah's eyes fluttered open. "Water," he mumbled.

Henry held a tin cup to his lips. "Easy now. You're safe."

"Thought...thought...over," he whispered, eyes closed.

"Well, the Good Lord answered your prayers, because I know you were praying something fierce with that bear breathing down your neck."

A weak smile flitted across his face as his head fell back onto the burlap bag pillow.

"Sleep good for him now," Ortega said, taking the cup from Henry.

Henry stood stiffly.

James and Gideon sat nearby, cleaning and oiling their revolvers and rifles. Michael stood in the rain, just beyond the tarp.

Ortega motioned to Michael. "Get back under here now; get that leg up."

Michael crawled up to Josiah and lay down next to him. Ortega began to put a fresh dry dressing on his legs. Wizzy sat quietly under the wagon listening, trying to keep his head dry until his scalp healed.

James studied the wagon of wounded. How much longer? he wondered. How much longer?

Great Bear wandered north for two days with no destination in mind. The ache in his head throbbed constantly, so he had no clear thought or definite idea about what he was doing. It might have been instinct or some other primitive sense leading him on. He followed no trails. At one point he crawled up the side of a steep hill through an ancient forest to an old, moss-covered cave. Through his clouded and injured mind, he had found his way back to the cave where he was born.

But it was occupied.

The magnificent silver-back grizzly, in his prime, walked out and stood, growling threateningly.

Great Bear also stood, head arched downward, clawed paws out to the sides at the ready. He was easily twice as large and twice as heavy.

They stood like that, growling fiercely and swiping without making contact. Suddenly, the grizzly turned and ran. Great Bear started to give chase but stopped, watching the bear run down the mountain. He roared, then turned and entered the cave and lay down. He had lived in this cave the first year of his life, before they had to move. He could not remember why. The ceiling was black from human fires from some time in the distant past. Figures drawn in charcoal decorated the walls, showing hunting scenes with bison, sloths, lions, mammoths with long curved tusks, and camels. Although the grizzly smell lingered, to him it still smelled of home. A sense of peace settled on his troubled heart and mind, and he slept for two days straight. His breathing was so shallow, anyone happening upon the cave might have thought he had died.

"Well, for the last three days, we've been all over this mountain range," Robert said. "I think he's moved on."

The men were finishing breakfast and handing their plates to Whipple.

James nodded his head approvingly. "I supposed it is time to go."

"There is not enough room for a good ambush at the cave," Henry said. "Not enough cover for us."

"We have to get the bear down the hill," Gideon said. Josiah sat next to him listening, but did not add his thoughts. He had not spoken much since his near-death encounter with the bear. He did not yet "feel right." Juan Ortega assured him that the blow to the head would take longer to heal than broken bones, so just be patient. That was okay with him. He sat, back against the wagon wheel, eyes closed, but listened to the debate about what to do.

"The bear has disappeared for a few days before," James said. "We can't let our guard down."

"Aye, that one is uncanny fast and sneaky as a leprechaun," O'Keefe said knowingly. "If'n you let your guard down, he'll be on you like Henry on Juan's biscuits with bacon gravy."

The men laughed.

"Well, everyone knows I'm partial to bacon," Henry explained with a wry grin.

"The only place for a good ambush is that open area down the hill from the cave, where we set up camp the night of the storm," James said. That was when they were bringing the cattle up from San Antonio and camped by the river when the tornado swept down the valley. The vaqueros had died near there.

"There's room enough for good fighting positions, and we can build traps," Robert said.

O'Keefe said, "Let's dig a big pit with spikes or spears in the bottom, so if nothin' else works, the brute will fall in there and impale himself."

"Great idea," Robert said.

"Stake a cow nearby," James said. "To sort of draw him in."

"I wish we had more shovels," Robert said.

"True," James agreed. "The two will have to do, but we can take turns.

Whipple walked up and dropped the two shovels by the firepit and a wooden bucket.

"What's the bucket for?" Robert asked.

"For liftin' dirt out of the pit," Whipple replied, as if it was obvious.

Robert studied him for a slow count of two. "That's a mighty fine suggestion, Whipple."

The boy just shrugged and walked away.

Robert looked at James.

James said, "He might be slow, but he's thinking ahead."

Robert looked around at Whipple. Maybe he wasn't as simple as they thought. Or maybe, he was getting better after all this time. When Whipple was thirteen, a horse threw him out of the corral and into the water trough. All of the onlookers had laughed at the unfortunate accident. And everyone thought the other person would rescue him from the water. But almost three minutes passed before someone realized Whipple was still under. They got him breathing again, but he was never quite the same rambunctious boy he had once been.

Henry hefted the pick to his shoulder.

James stood next to him. "We'll need guards out watching for the bear, and maybe Philip or Michael further out."

Gideon picked up the other shovel.

"I want to move the herd closer," Robert said. "Close to the ambush site, but out of the trees, or on the edge of the trees."

239

"Some risky," James said. "But sure. Makes sense." He was thinking about how they were spread out before the Indians attacked. The idea of leaving for home had slipped away in the plan to trap the bear. He knew he could probably talk them into leaving, but the group seemed to have rallied to finish the job.

"Well, let's get up there and work out the details," Henry said.

The outline in the dirt was twelve feet by twelve feet square. The digging was easy at first; the top two feet of loose forest soil gave easily under the steady shovels. But then the compacted, hard clay and rock began, and Henry stepped in with his pick to break it up. They worked around the clock, not knowing how much time they really had. After one full day, the pit was twelve feet square and eight feet deep.

"I'm impressed," James said.

"It's this metal bar Ortega gave us," Henry said from down in the pit. His shirt was off and his sweaty skin was covered in a thin gray and brown dust. He held the metal bar Ortega used for a large animal on the spit above the fire. "With this bar I can chisel away at the hard dirt, then we throw it out with the shovel or use Whipple's bucket there. Between Emilio on the pick and me with the bar, we are making short work of it."

O'Keefe and Gideon never stopped shoveling during this conversation.

"How deep should we make the pit?" Henry asked.

"Deep enough so he doesn't fall in and then quickly climb out."

"So, what—twenty feet?" Henry smiled at the thought of needing a ladder to get out. He almost did now. They had cut two-foot-wide stairs into the dirt on one side to get out, that they would cut away when done.

On the pit edge, Rhodes held the rope and bucket. "But if he's stabbed by the spears, wouldn't that mean the pit only needs to be about this deep?" Rhodes asked, surveying the pit around him.

James chuckled. "It's about eight feet now. Even if the bear is speared, he could hop out of this shallow pit and tear into us, angrier than ever. But if the pit is deep enough, and he is not mortally wounded, we can run up here and fire down on him before he gets out, if he's able."

"So probably twelve feet deep?" Henry suggested. James shook his head.

"Fifteen feet?" Thomas Rhodes said. James shook his head.

He studied the pit and thought about the bear. "I would say fifteen at a minimum. Twenty would be better." Twenty feet deep would suit him fine, although fifteen would probably work, if the stakes did their job. Maybe they should just keep digging until the bear showed up. But then Henry and Emilio would complain they were being used as bait. He smiled at the thought, but only with his eyes.

Henry frowned sideways and began stabbing the pit floor with the pike.

James started to leave then turned back. "Stop digging if you hit water." Henry gave him a short chuckle to acknowledge the idea but never stopped working.

After another day of round-the-clock digging, the pit was eighteen feet deep. Mainly because when they reached fifteen feet, it was James' and Gideon's turn to dig at midnight, and they dug furiously until morning with Whipple and Rhodes pulling up buckets of dirt. And they did need the pole ladder Robert made the day before.

Gideon and O'Keefe planted twelve spears in the bottom by digging holes with Henry's bar. During the digging, other people had cut down narrow aspen and poplar. These were woven with thin branches to form a platform, then carefully pulled into position and centered over the pit.

James rubbed his chin. "I think the platform will barely hold a person but not that bear."

"Want to test it?" Henry asked, smiling.

"Too dangerous," James said not getting the joke at first. "I don't think anyone should test it." He could think of a dozen reasons why someone might want to step out over the pit, and all had something to do with luring the bear into the trap.

James said, "I'm going to sling a rope across the pit. Tie one end on that stump over there—up the hill, and the other end around that little tree on the far side."

"Why you doin' that?" Robert asked.

Henry said, "In case he wants to walk out onto the platform. If it starts to collapse under him, he can grab the rope on the way down."

James nodded to Henry. "Exactly."

"You do know that for this big bear, that pit ain't that deep," Robert said, standing on the edge. "If'n the bear falls in with you hangin' from the rope, he'll be able to grab you."

"Once the bear is in the pit, you'd be dangling there like a hog on the spit, within easy reachin' distance," O'Keefe said. "Why he'd pluck you off that rope like a ripe grape off the vine."

James shrugged. "If that's how it works out, I'll keep that in mind. Could be someone else is out there, not me. It's just for safety, anyhow."

While digging the pit, others worked on fighting positions, some on the ground, two others in nearby trees. With the axe, Thomas was able to fashion crude boards from the felled trees. O'Keefe used them up in two trees to fashion platforms for a shooter.

"When I was a kid, I built a platform like this'n up in the old oak tree by our house," O'Keefe said. "Pretendin' we was pirates up in the crow's nest, looking for merchant ships to plunder."

"What's a crow's nest?" Marcus asked.

"Now picture in your mind a big ship of the sea with tall white sails brushin' the fluffy clouds above," O'Keefe said seriously, forming the outline of a tall ship with his hands. "At the very top, where the lines bind the spars and sail riggin' together, there sits a wee box for the look out—the crow's nest, like what a crow might build at the top of a tall tree for her eggs. The captain sends a lad up the ropes to the box, and he reports what sights come to hand. The lad might cry out, *Land ho!* for sightin' land; or, *Thar she blows!* for a whale; or, *Ahoy mateys, sails two points to starboard,* for another ship to the front right. You get the idea."

"Aye, matey," Marcus replied sharply. "I do at that."

"Now you're talkin', lad. I see I'm makin' a good impression on you. When you finally go to sea, you'll already speak the language, proper like, and know what all is goin' on. Now, fetch me that other board."

J.C. Graves

CHAPTER NINETEEN

After five days, James and the others stood next to the pit and studied their handiwork.

"I don't know what else we can do," Henry said.

James nodded with satisfaction. "Well, if we think of anything, we can fine-tune the ambush until the bear decides to pay us a social call."

"The bear is just plain ornery and unsociable to keep us waiting and guessing what he'll do next," Josiah said. He had not helped to prepare. He spent his days sitting under a tree, usually with Wizzy, watching the men work. His head didn't hurt anymore, but whenever he tried to help, headaches started and his strength drained out of him like water out of a lead shot bucket.

Robert said, "Why don't we stake the cow?"

"And blow the trumpet once in a while," Wizzy added. He had grown fairly proficient in its use.

"Yes, and blow the trumpet maybe a few times per hour," James said. "During the day."

"The critter could come at any time," Robert noted. "Would be most convenient if'n he came around when we were all set up and ready like." He paused, tilting his hat back. "But it ain't likely to happen that way, is it?"

"Day would be better, but he will probably come after dark," Thomas said.

"He's plumb smart, that one," O'Keefe said knowingly.

James looked off to the north. "Michael and Philip are watching the trails. If they don't get jumped, we should have a little warning."

"True," Gideon said, "But they are not out there at night."

Ortega had set up a rope with cans at the cave entrance and at various likely avenues of approach coming down the hill. "Since the bear moves through the forest like a ghost, the cans will sig__," Ortega explained.

Late that afternoon, Michael and Philip rode in for supper. "Not a sign of him," Michael said. He sounded disappointed.

Josiah handed Philip and Michael each a plate. "I wonder if he left the country or died or something. That would be nice." He sat back down by the fire and opened his King James bible.

Philip nodded to the south. "Storm coming."

CHAPTER TWENTY

The first sprinkles began to hit the dry ground around two in the morning, when a band of light rain passed through.

O'Keefe rode in from guarding the herd. "James."

James immediately sat up in his blankets. "What is it?" He was dressed, boots and all.

"Thought you should know, lightnin' comin'."

As if in answer to the question, off to the south a streak of lightning flashed to the ground, the thunder answering ten seconds later.

Without a word, James carried his saddle to the remuda and found his black horse. It nickered and tossed its head in anticipation of a night ride.

Henry walked up with his saddle. "Last thing we need is for the herd to run into the pit."

"Would be a sorry sight. It's just about big enough to hold the whole bunch."

"Do you want everyone up?" Henry asked.

During the cattle drive, with over three thousand cattle milling around, they needed only six men out on the herd in a night storm, while the others slept under or around the wagon, trying to stay dry. Now they had a little herd of only forty-eight cattle. But James did not want them to run into the pit or run around the mountain where the bear could attack the unwary drover. Would be better to have more people out working the cattle in the dark than deal with the aftermath the next day, especially if the cattle felt compelled to depart the area.

Gideon, Washington and Emilio were in the defensive positions around the pit. James walked his horse over to them and explained about the storm and the herd.

Gideon said, "Why don't we all saddle up to control the herd in the storm and worry about the bear another time." He did not anticipate a bear attack in the morning dark. He liked the idea that Josiah had killed it, even if they might never know for sure.

James looked around. "Might as well."

Ortega's lantern hung on a hook by the wagon seat, casting a dim light over the area. Emilio climbed down from the tree, stretched, and walked over to the wagon to get his saddle.

Gideon stood, stretching the cold and damp out of his muscles. "Priorities."

"Can't see much anyhow, what with the storm movin' in," Washington said. "That patchy rain earlier really knocked down our perimeter fires."

The bear lay at the edge of the tree line, watching the perimeter fires until the first rain nearly put them out. He knew where two people sat in a dugout position, rifles at the ready, watching warily. Another person lay in the tree stand off to the right. A lone cow stood staked to the ground by the middle fire. He turned his gaze to the right. Off to the south the lightning increased until it was a constant show, either dancing to the ground or flitting from cloud to cloud above. A thunderhead towered high into the sky, illuminated by the flashes of light, slowly descending on the scene.

The constant ache in his head weighed him down. He desired the humans, but for the first time he seemed almost detached and able to decide when to attack—not driven by madness. He was an experienced, patient hunter, able to stay still in one spot for hours before springing his trap and attacking. He *would* attack.

Yellow snot dribbled out his nose in a constant flow and his tongue hung down languidly. His fur had become matted in areas, and course and stiff in others. The vibrant sheen of a well-groomed, healthy coat had long since disappeared. His breathing came in long wheezing pants, and his eyes appeared cloudy.

He was dying.

Somewhere in his being, he felt his time was short, and welcomed it. He knew things had not been right with him since the puny creature shot his head. But while the end might be near, his perpetual and unending madness needed to be fed. He sensed that this attack would be his last, then he would lie down to sleep for the last time, like so many of his ancestors before him, and depart the land forever.

Like a tidal wave breaking over the forest, the wall of rain came in a sudden inundating wave.

"Thar she blows!" Marcus hollered from his horse. A sudden gust of wind blew his hat away into the darkness and he cried out, angry with himself. He had forgotten to tighten the chin strap, and there was no chance of finding it now. Maybe in the morning—in the next state.

Everyone was up and in the saddle. Ortega and Whipple sat in the wagon, watching out the back and catching streams of fresh water in buckets and cans to fill the main water barrel. Josiah and Wizzy sat in the back, behind them.

"Looks like a bad storm," Josiah said, looking out the front flap. He felt uneasy. "Wizzy, let's get our horses and be ready for whatever happens."

James eased his horse alongside the herd, talking calmly to the cattle. He could hear O'Keefe on the other side, singing a lusty ballad. Most of the others just sat their horses, watching, waiting for something or nothing to happen. James noticed Emilio's head bobbing, probably asleep. He wasn't officially on duty.

Twenty minutes later, lightning struck the tree just beyond the wagon and the race commenced. The little herd surged north, narrowly missing the wagon. James and the others rode alongside, shouting and trying to turn them around. Someone fired a revolver. A rifle sounded.

And then a roar.

When the lightning hit the tree not fifty feet from him, Great Bear stood up on all fours in sudden fear. One minute he had been studying the group down the hill in

255

front of him, in a detached half sleep, and the next he only wanted to destroy and eat these invaders of his precious territory.

He charged down the hill, ears laid flat against his skull, narrowly missing the pit and attacked the little herd as it surged by. His claws raked along the sides and flanks of the cows, who bellowed in pain and surprise. He stood on two feet, wheeling around, just as a horse ran into him. Someone shouted in surprise, as they flew through the air. Cattle brushed by. A horn pierced his side and he swung his long claws around, lacerating the unfortunate cow.

Emilio lay in the mud just beyond the bear. Like a rock in the river, the bear stood in the vortex, keeping the herd from trampling him. But the herd was small and soon passed. He scrambled to his feet and ran after the cows. At the first rider he found, he shouted. "The bear! He is here!"

Washington T. Jefferson reined in. Over the thunder and rain storm, he shouted, "The bear is where?"

"Here! Here!" Emilio shouted, clutching desperately at Jefferson's stirrup. "Let me up!"

Washington pulled him up behind the saddle.

Lighting hit the ground down the hill, and Washington saw the bear lumbering toward them. "Hold on tight!" He put spurs to horse and shot away.

Whipple looked out the back of the wagon at the lightning strike. "That was a close one."

Before the lightning strike, Josiah and Wizzy had found their horses and were now following the herd, despite orders from James and Robert to stay in the wagon. "It's been most of two weeks," Wizzy had complained. "I can't stay put forever." Thomas Rhodes had fashioned him a skull cap out of cowhide and worked cooking oil into the pores. He figured that if Wizzy had to get his head wet before he should, he could wear the cap for some protection. It was scraped so thin, Wizzy could wear his regular hat.

Although the rain fell like a waterfall, Ortega dropped to the ground. "Stay in the wagon, Whipple. I check my mules."

As he suspected, they had broken loose. Probably running along with the cattle and the remuda. He frowned and walked down the hill. He could hear the cattle and drovers out in front somewhere, but he couldn't see a thing. He had to be careful not to get run down by someone.

Great Bear watched the horse with two people bolt away and stopped, sitting heavily. A low, rumbling growl started deep in his chest. Through the heavy downpour, he had caught the faint scent of humans, the abject fear radiating from them. It pleased him. He could hear the cattle moving north. Off to his left something caught his attention. He stood and lumbered slowly in that direction.

The bear walked up to the back of the wagon. On all fours, he could easily peer into the back. A shadow passed in front of the lantern and drool began to flow out of the corners of his mouth.

Whipple heard a huffing sound and turned. The lantern lit the face of the monster bear only feet from him, and he screamed like a girl, high and piercing and heart felt.

The bear lunged.

Whipple fell back, barely avoiding the snapping jaws, his hands on the bear's nose, pushing desperately, his feet kicking the bear's ears.

The bear put its front feet onto the back of the wagon. The front of the wagon tipped up. Whipple began to slide toward the bear and reached out to grab something to hold on to. He kicked the bear's nose with his left foot and kicked the bag of flour with the other. White powder filled the air. The bear roared, spittle flying. In the flour and confusion, the bear stepped back and the wagon dropped. Whipple started to stand and fell backward into the tailgate.

Suddenly, the bear's great head thrust into the back of the wagon again, only Whipple was under the bear's chin, his body covered in white flour, eyes bugging out with horror. Flour dust filled the air. Whipple held his breath, hands over mouth, hoping the bear would not see him. The bear peeled the tailgate off the wagon with his claws and started to climb in, when it noticed Whipple lying right under him. He reared back and roared in triumph.

As he lunged at Whipple, the lantern hit his nose, glass cracking, and the bear's head burst into flame. The bear fell back, swiping at his face in anger and confusion. He had no experience with fire, and it burned mercilessly. Ortega had taken the cap off the side where the oil was poured in, so a little oil had splashed across the bear's face as the lantern broke.

Ortega came around the outside and pulled Whipple out of the wagon by his shoulders, the bear only feet away. The young man was unconscious and limp.

"Stand up, damn you!" Ortega shouted into his face. "Or bear eat you!" Whipple did not respond.

Ortega dragged him past the front of the wagon, trying to get as far away as possible before the bear came after them. Wait! The long rifles were in the wagon—and loaded. He dropped Whipple in the mud by the wagon tongue. He climbed up the front and into the wagon. Small flames of burning kerosene licked the canvas at the back, starting to spread, but he knew the rifles were in their scabbards on the left side. He reached down, found one and pulled it up. He threw off the leather scabbard and cocked the hammer.

The bear roared and lunged forward, stepping on the wagon again. The back of the wagon dropped and the front pitched up into the air.

As Ortega's feet left the floor boards, he fired the large Enfield rifle, a grim smile on his face. The hammer fell. But without a percussion cap, no fire found the little chamber of black powder. He choked out a desperate, gurgling scream. Before him, the great bear's head filled the back of the wagon, smoke curling up from singed fur, the red eyes glowing, the mouth open wide in anticipation, and the long yellow teeth gleaming in the flickering flames.

As Ortega flopped onto the bear's face, it threw him to the ground and tore into his frail body. Not eating. Just tearing and shredding with teeth and claws, parts

260

flying everywhere, some up to fifty feet away. Great Bear wanted to destroy the one who had caused him such agonizing pain. Finally, he slurped up the liver and turned toward his cave.

James thought he heard a loud noise behind him, but he was about to throw a loop over the cow leading the frightened herd down the hill. When the lightning flashed, he caught the cow and pulled her to the left. She fought briefly, tossing and twisting her head, dragging his horse around, then settled in to follow. Lightning continued to flit across the clouds above, lighting up the area. The rain pounded steadily, and the thunder rumbled continuously. He looked south. Was that a roar he heard or just more lightning and thunder?

The herd finally fell into a walk behind the cow, the riders pushing the strays into the group. A cold stream of water fell off the back of his hat and down his shirt, so he hitched up his coat collar. He thought Ortega would soon have a good fire going and Whipple would get a fresh pot of coffee on. If the rain let up some, maybe they would all dry out by morning. Must be about five, he thought. Won't be leaving today. But they would sure leave tomorrow, hell or high water.

He noticed Washington Jefferson letting Emilio drop to the ground from the back of his horse.

"Lose your horse?" James asked, riding up. "That's unusual for you."

"The bear!" Emilio shouted.

Without a word James dropped the rope leading the cow and charged back to camp. He cursed himself for chasing the herd; he couldn't be more than a half mile away. He spurred the black stallion, urging more speed, even though the muddy ground could prove fatal in a fall. The horse seemed to understand and flattened out into a ground pounding dash.

The rain was blinding, but the continuous flashes of lightning lit up the mountain, so they could avoid obstacles. He noticed a flickering light. The back of the chuck wagon seemed to be on fire. And there was the bear, walking away from the wagon. He had never seen it plainly, out in the open, and the creature's size astounded him, even with a partial glimpse in the storm. How could it possibly be so big? It was at least four times the size of his stallion. Bigger.

James pulled out the Henry rifle, levered in a round and rode right at the bear. Big or not, enough lead would eventually kill it, he thought, starting with his first contribution. He fired.

The bear spun around with surprising speed and agility. James pulled the reins with his left hand, veering his stallion away while firing the big rifle with only his right. The bear was too big and too close to miss.

But the bear did not stand still. It charged with blinding speed. James thought he had given the bear a wide enough berth, but it was on him in a second. He flipped the rifle to chamber a round with one hand and fired a third time. The bear hit the horse, and James flew through the air. He landed hard, sliding in the mud on his back for twenty feet. He jumped up, hat and rifle missing. His stallion jumped to its feet and bolted, leaving James standing alone.

The bear stood, looking left and right, then spotted him and charged. James ran for his life but knew he was going to die a violent terrible death. Suddenly, his feet dropped out from under him, but a rope caught under his right arm. Even in the dark, he knew he had run into the bear pit, but the safety rope had saved him from being impaled on the spears below.

In a full charge, eyes on his intended victim, the bear suddenly plunged into the pit.

Hand over hand, James pulled himself to the pit edge and out. In the east, the horizon had begun to lighten, but he could not see into the pit. He stood at the edge, waiting for another lightning strike. Finally, the lightning flashed between the clouds above. He expected to see the bear lying in the pit, like a pin cushion, with at least ten spears imbedded in its body. Instead, the monster bear stood, looking up at him, no more than six feet away. Fear swept through him and he involuntarily stepped back.

Because the bear flew into the pit on an angle and at high speed, most of the upward pointing spears were knocked aside. Two spears punctured his side, creating superficial wounds. Then to James' utter surprise, the bear lunged forward, grabbed the upper edge of the pit—eighteen feet high, and swiftly pulled himself out. James fell back, the bear's dark menacing frame towering above him.

He was right, he thought. The pit should have been twenty feet deep—no, thirty.

The bear leaned forward, roaring mightily, prepared to pounce on his prey, when Henry's horse slammed into it. Bear, horse and Henry tumbled back into the pit. The horse screamed with a broken front left leg. In the pit, the bear stood and bit down viciously on the horse's neck, ripping out a great chunk; the horse's scream cut off suddenly.

James jumped to the edge of the pit, trying to peer into the darkness, when the great shaggy head reared up out of the darkness and looked him in the eyes—again.

He could not see Henry and wondered at his fate, but he turned and ran toward the wagon. He heard a great huff and did not need to look around; he knew the bear was out of the pit, and after him.

The rain thickened, but the sky continued to grow lighter. Gideon's horse slid to a stop in the mud, squatted on its back haunches, nearly falling. He stood on his toes in the stirrups and fired his Henry as fast as he could chamber a round. Robert arrived and fired his Henry rifle from the downhill side of the pit. James fell, sliding on his stomach, but the bear had just turned toward Gideon. Although Gideon emptied his Henry rifle into the bear, none of the sixteen bullets were lethal. Great Bear was bleeding from over twenty wounds, but they only magnified his immense rage and madness. He charged Gideon.

Gideon could not believe what he was seeing. How could a brute that big, move that fast? He turned his horse to escape. Although the big horse dug in its hooves and the mud flew, he seemed to make no progress in the wet mud. The bear swept the horses' rear legs away and bit down viciously on the right haunch. The horse screamed. Gideon screamed, the bear's biting jaws just inches away, as they all collapsed to the ground.

Robert continued to fire, steam rising from the rifle barrel.

While the bear mauled his horse, Gideon lay quietly with his left leg pinned under the horse, his eyes tightly closed. Hell of a way to die, he thought.

The bear finally noticed Gideon and crept closer, licking its lips.

When a wad of bloody saliva coated his face, Gideon opened his eyes, blurred by the slobber. The bear loomed over him, muzzle less than twelve inches away. Then one of Robert's bullets hit the bear on the side of the head and it spun around. Again, it roared, spittle and bloody foam flying.

Josiah stopped his horse by James. He dismounted, took a knee and began firing, his rifle leveled over his splinted left arm.

The bear spun back toward Josiah and James, only forty feet away and charged. Robert reloaded.

Emilio had found his horse, or his horse found him. He flew by the charging bear and threw the lariat neatly around the bear's neck, pulling it off balance and over onto its back. "That is for José and Raul!" he shouted. He quickly dallied the rope around the saddle horn, urging his horse to drag the brute down the hill in the mud.

The bear stood. The horse stopped, jerked around so suddenly that Emilio flew out of the saddle again, landing hard and breaking his neck.

As the bear purposefully descended on Emilio's corpse to eat it, Philip Two Feathers rode up, stood on his saddle, and dived onto the bear's great back. While holding a tuft of hair with his left hand, he thrust his long knife into the neck repeatedly. The bear reached around with its right claws and swept Philip around to the front and bit off his head, swallowing it.

Robert and Josiah were both reloading furiously, while James, kneeling on his left knee, fired his revolvers. He got off seven shots before the rain soaked the powder in the other cylinders.

Great Bear turned back to the flickering fire on the wagon. Overwhelming madness filled his raving mind with blood lust and the need to kill everything in sight. In the light of the burning wagon, two figures huddled close together in front, firing the annoying bullets at him. One bullet cut his ear. He roared in anger, not in pain, and charged again.

As he careened toward Josiah and James like a giant cannonball, a loud boom came from the direction of the wagon, behind them.

Great Bear fell on his face and slid the last twenty feet. James reached out a shaking hand and touched the bear's bloody muzzle. The bear's black eyes stared back at him. Even in death, they seemed to be filled with wrath and evil. With a final heave and shake, the bear took its last breath and sighed out a cloud of warm vapor.

"Oh my God," Josiah whispered, shaking uncontrollably. He fell back from his knees into a seated position. "Are you okay, James?" he asked with trembling voice.

James gulped. "I...I think I just aged twenty years this morning."

Michael walked up, extending a hand. He pulled James to his feet then Josiah.

James noticed Michael holding his Whitworth sharpshooter rifle.

"Nice rifle," Michael said, handing it to him. "Dead on."

James looked back down at the bear. In the growing light, he could just make out a neat hole between the eyes, a thin seep of blood oozing out. "You certainly saved our lives. All of us, I think."

Robert freed Gideon from under his dead horse, then threw a loop into the pit and used his horse to drag out

Henry, battered and shaken—three broken ribs, but otherwise healthy.

The sky continued to lighten, and the rain finally put out the wagon fire. O'Keefe tended Whipple, who seemed to have a concussion. Others reverently gathered up what they could find of old Juan Ortega.

From in the saddle, Robert said, "I want to save the hide—head, feet, everythin'. No one will ever believe our story otherwise."

"Have at it," James said with a I-don't-care wave of his hand. He grabbed Henry around the shoulders, who grabbed Gideon and they walked back to the wagon. Josiah and Michael followed, hands around their shoulders.

By late morning, the rain died down to a sprinkle then stopped. Just before noon, the sun broke through the clouds, causing the ground to give up a foggy steam as it warmed.

Two hours later, Thomas Rhodes brought the bear's skull up to the roaring fire and set it down. Between the bear's left ear hole and eye socket, sat the black flint arrowhead, sticking up a quarter inch.

"I think this is what made the bear so mean," Thomas said.

James tried to pull it out with his hand, but it remained firmly wedged in the bone. He retrieved the horseshoeing pliers from the wagon, and pulled and wiggled the arrowhead until it worked loose. Yellow-green puss dripped off the long tip and smelled disgusting. He walked around the group with the bloody skull and held up the flint arrowhead for everyone to inspect.

Henry inspected the skull and said, "Some fool shot this poor bear in the head and the rampage started. Whoever shot him was probably the first of many to die by the bear's madness."

"Looky here at this," O'Keefe announced. He and five others stretched out the hide. "I count seventy-six holes from bullets, spears and arrows through his hide. But he had a thick layer of muscle and fat and thick bones, so only a shot to the head or heart could really kill him."

Gideon said, "From the hide we figured him at sixteen feet tall." They had also recovered Philip's head from the stomach, and Juan's right hand—confirmed by the big silver and turquoise ring—but no one wanted to talk about that.

"Well, the old varmint is at peace now," Robert said wistfully.

Josiah frowned, shaking his head sadly. "Must be the last of his kind." Now that the beast was dead and his long life certain—hopefully, he could entertain more philosophical ideas. The thought that the great bear had been suffering the whole time, also put a damper on their celebrations, his in particular. He had a sermon planned about the demon-possessed bear, which would now need some revision.

The bear's entrails were thrown into the pit. It took them eight hours to fill it in. They buried Ortega and Emilio and Philip Two Feathers back up in the tree line, their graves looking out over the beautiful river valley below and the vista of green prairie grass beyond. Josiah led the service, ending with *Amazing Grace*.

The somber group started back to the Don Pedro rancho outside San Antonio early the next morning.

J.C. Graves

CHAPTER TWENTY-ONE

F ar up on the ridge, the Cheyenne Shaman watched the lonely band until they disappeared in the distance. He slid off his horse, letting it stand quietly, waiting. He walked to the ledge in front of the cave and performed the bear dance, chanting and singing until well after dark. The dance and song were plaintive and haunting. He did not call on Great Bear to intervene in tribal affairs anymore. Instead, his song carried with it the weeping of the ages at the passing of Great Brother, the protector and guide of the People. He lit a fire just inside the cave. After a few hours he used the burnt coal to draw pictures of Great Bear and his story.

Great Bear lived in peace, content, then people came—stick figures, dancing in the light of his little smokeless fire. He drew a Cheyenne warrior attacking Great Bear. Then another scene of Great Bear surrounded by humans, attacking him with guns, arrows, and spears. Other animals stood beyond, watching the epic battle, but their heads were bowed, because they were weeping. When he finished, he stood back. Tears fell unhindered; his frown permanently etched into his brown leathery face. He took a deep breath and turned. He kicked dirt over the fire and jumped on his horse. In the back of his mind, he knew something profound had happened; that the world at large had changed forever. He sat looking out over the dark, moon lit prairie and knew that the People's way of life would be over in only a matter of years—in his lifetime. Great Bear and his kind were gone, and so the People who worshipped and honored him would soon follow.

The End

Coming Soon
Death is a Sharpshooter

Made in the USA
Monee, IL
07 March 2020